LOVE
TORNADO

Also By Mable John and David Ritz

Sanctified Blues

Stay Out of the Kitchen!

LOVE TORNADO

A NOVEL

MABLE JOHN AND
DAVID RITZ

Broadway Books
New York

Copyright © 2008 by Mable John and David Ritz

All Rights Reserved

Published in the United States by Broadway Books, an imprint of The Doubleday Publishing Group, a division of Random House, Inc., New York.
www.broadwaybooks.com

Broadway Books and its logo, a letter B bisected on the diagonal, are trademarks of Random House, Inc.

Book design by Caroline Cunningham

Library of Congress Cataloging-in-Publication Data
John, Mable.
    Love tornado / by Mable John and David Ritz. —
        p. cm.
    1. African Americans—Fiction. 2. African American musicians—Fiction.
    3. Domestic fiction. I. Ritz, David. II. Title.

PS3610.O26L68 2008
813'.6—dc22

2007045099

978-0-7679-2167-1

146866421

For my children and for my church, Joy in Jesus,

which has allowed me to explore this

beautiful world of writing

POSTCARDS FROM GOD

ALBERTINA," my friend Justine asks me, "do you really think the Lord is sending you postcards?"

"It's just a figure of speech," I say, "but yes, I always feel Him communicating with me."

"Even here in Hawaii in June when everyone's running around practically naked?"

"Especially here in Hawaii where His natural wonders take my breath away. Everywhere I look, I see Him."

"Well, everywhere I look, I see hot men."

"You're a married woman now, Justine."

"*Happily* married woman," Justine adds. "But that don't mean I've gone blind. Like you say, this is a state of beautiful sights. And when it comes to beautiful men, I'm always in a state of excitement."

"Overexcitement," I'd say.

"Albertina," says Justine, "you've had your own excitement

in that area. Why just last year, you had *two* mules kicking in your stall."

I can't help but laugh. In some sense Justine is right. Clifford Bloom and Mario Pani had both proposed marriage. But looking out at the gorgeous orange-red-pink-blue sunset from Justine's house high on a cliff in the Honolulu suburb of Kahala, all that drama feels like a lifetime ago. Clifford has moved to Dallas, and Mario understands that friendship, not marriage, is far more suitable to my lifestyle.

For now I can concentrate on the sunset and the sea.

For now I can soak up God's beauty.

"Do you mind if I pray?" I ask Justine.

"Lemme take another sip of this margarita," she replies. "That'll warm up my holy ghost."

"Father God," I say, ignoring Justine's last remark and taking her hand, "we thank You for this moment. We thank You for keeping us in this moment. We thank You for Your son and the miracle of His being in our hearts—His *being* our hearts—every moment of every day. We praise You and glorify You, God, for bringing us a mighty long way. What a wonder You are! You allow us to live lives that are forever changing, forever surprising. You allow us to grow and You allow us to know You more intimately, through our triumphs and through our struggles. They all bring us closer to You, Father God—the victories, the defeats, the pain, the joy—they all serve to remind us that You are our strength, our hope, our life. We see You in the sky, Father God, and we see You in the sea. We see You in each other's eyes. We see You when we close our eyes, when we sleep at night, and when we walk through the dark woods and walk on the sunlit beaches. We love how You stay with us, Father, how You whisper love in our ears, how You breathe us, bathe us in Your grace. We give You praise and we give You honor. We bow our heads and simply say, 'Thank You, thank You for this life, thank You for this moment.' In Jesus' precious name, Amen."

"Girlfriend," says Justine, "you sure do know how to pray. We should package those prayers and sell 'em at the mall."

My mind is still on the Lord.

"You listening to me, Albertina?" Justine asks.

"Baby," I say, "I hardly have a choice."

Just then Justine's husband arrives. Ken Kawika is a short, handsome brown-skinned man who speaks with an island accent and indulges his wife shamelessly. He's a successful singer who performs at many of the hotels on Waikiki Beach. This is his second marriage. He's thrilled to have found someone as lively and unpredictable as Justine.

Justine has found work as a merchandise manager at the local Wal-Mart, where the pace is several beats behind Los Angeles. Despite the fact that her new husband makes good money, Justine wants to remain independent. I give her credit for that.

Ken is cooking an exotic pork dish he learned from his mother, who had been the personal cook of the owner of a great pineapple plantation on the island. He sings an enchanting Hawaiian melody as he busies himself in the kitchen with the elaborate preparations.

"You gals let me know if you need anything," he offers. "I'll have the appetizers out in just a sec."

"You've struck gold with that man," I tell Justine.

"He's a sweetheart," says Justine. "And I love him dearly. But he does tire quickly."

I leave the last remark alone.

Fortunately Justine changes the topic. "I wish you were staying a few more days."

"I promised the church I'd be back for Sunday's service."

Justine raises her eyebrows. "Sounds like a blast," she says.

"These last three days with you have been beautiful," I tell her. "I couldn't have asked for a more restful vacation."

"If only we had found you a man . . ."

"I found what I was looking for a long time ago, baby," I say.

Justine cuts me off and says, "I'm going to find that reality show I was telling you about, Albertina. The one where five sex-crazed women get on an island to go after three men and battle it out for—"

"I could skip that one."

Justine turns on the set anyway and starts clicking the remote.

I suddenly see the face of my godson, J Love.

"Hold it there, Justine! That's my boy!"

"That rapper?"

"He's rapping for the Lord."

Justine accidentally hit on the Word Channel, the cable station that broadcasts preachers and gospel singers. J Love is up in front of the congregation of a megachurch and has the saints going crazy.

I see he's gotten taller. Last year when I saw J he must have been five foot six. Now he looks like he's shot up to five foot ten or eleven. At fifteen, he looks even younger. He has a baby face and sparkling dark-brown eyes. He's skinny as a pole and flashes his smile in a way that makes you love him. Plus he moves like quicksilver. Ever since he was a little boy he has been a brilliant dancer. He eyes the camera like it's his friend. There's not a shy bone in this boy's body.

"He's adorable," says Justine. "I'm just now realizing that's Shaleena Love's son, isn't it?"

"Sure enough is."

I knew Shaleena back when we were both Raelettes singing for Ray Charles. J is the spitting image of his beautiful mama. Over a strong hip-hop beat, J is saying,

Ain't none but the One
And One's all you need . . .
Yo, it ain't about bling and
And it ain't about greed
The One is your Father
Who had but one Son
And the Son is the One
Who can't be undone
He done saved us from sin
And sacrificed His All
Now let's hear His Word
Let's hear His call
He say, "My yoke is easy
My burden is light,
Just do My Father's will
And do it right
It's all as easy as one, two, three
Believe in My Father
Believe in Me
And when Holy Ghost comes down
Well, that makes three
Say, it's all easy as one, two, three
Believe in My Father
Believe in Me
And when Holy Ghost comes down
Well, that makes three
Let the church say—

It's all easy as one, two, three
Believe in My Father
Believe in Me
And when Holy Ghost comes down
Well, that makes three.

"I love his outfit," says Justine. "Haven't seen blue velvet harem pants since the days of MC Hammer."

"J always wears flashy clothes," I say. "Ever since he was a little boy. Always loved those sparkly shirts and those fancy sneakers."

"What's the 'J' stand for?"

"Julius Jay. His father was Julius Jay Turner, the fight promoter. But Julius never married Shaleena and never wanted to be bothered with his son."

"Wasn't Julius Turner killed in a shoot-out in Detroit?"

"Ten years ago. A fighter he had exploited went crazy on him and put a bullet through his head. I thank God Shaleena brought the boy up in Memphis, far from his father."

"She still staying in Memphis?"

"Works there as the music director at a private school," I explain. "Shaleena has a master's degree in music from Michigan State. She's done a beautiful job developing J's career and raising that boy alone."

"Hey," says Justine, pointing at the television, "isn't that the preacher who tried to buy your church last year?"

Sure enough. Bishop Henry Gold is shaking J's hand. Turns out the concert was videotaped at Gold's megachurch in Dallas, Texas.

"The kid's on the big gospel circuit," says Justine. "Must be making some good money. You worried about the world corrupting him, Albertina?"

"Not at all, baby. Shaleena has taught him good values. He's using his talent for the Lord and he's reaching young people. I'm proud of him, Justine, I really am."

That night, after a delicious dinner, I retire to Ken and Justine's guest room. I read my Bible and stop at a line from Psalm Twenty-six where David says, "O Lord, I love the habitation of Your house / And the place where your glory dwells." I feel I am in a place where His glory dwells. The window is open. The ocean breeze is fresh, cool, delightful. I close my eyes and thank God for the blessings of this moment, for the gift of prayer and rest.

But my sleep is not restful.

I wake up in the middle of the night. I am shaking and covered in sweat. I realize something has happened. I begin to remember a dream, a terrifying nightmare. It is about Shaleena Love. I am sure I dreamt about her because I just saw her son on television. But why was the dream so disturbing? Why in this dream did I hear the agonized cry of children? Why did I see mangled bodies? Why did I imagine Shaleena with her face contorted, her body maimed and lifeless?

"PERMIT THE CHILDREN TO COME TO ME"

PERMIT THE CHILDREN to come to me. That's what Jesus said," I tell the assembly of mourners. "They have come to Him. They are with Him. Our pain, our loss, our grief still overwhelm us. We remain numb, incredulous, devastated. But we know they are with Him. We do know that."

Never have I faced a more daunting task. I am in Memphis to minister to the parents of the eight children who were killed along with their teacher Shaleena Love.

I was awakened that night in Hawaii by Shaleena's spirit. Along with her students, she had experienced her transition that very night. They had been traveling by bus from Memphis to Nashville to perform for the governor of the state. Her choral group, consisting of eight ten-year-olds, had won recognition for their accomplishments. They had even recorded a CD of one of their concerts. That was the music being played under the words I spoke.

As I spoke, J sat next to me. He wasn't crying and he wasn't moving. His eyes stared out into space. His eyes were vacant. The boy was still in shock. When his mom's sister called me with the news, I immediately flew from Honolulu to Memphis, with a quick stopover in Chicago to meet J, who was in the middle of a tour with Kirk Franklin's gospel workshop. His aunt had called. But the woman, bless her heart, is a chronic drinker and drug user, and she was hysterical.

I assured J that indeed he was not alone. He was my godson. He was family, and he was not abandoned, not by any measure. At the same time I knew he felt abandoned—that, in fact, his mother had left this earth and there was no way now to make that awful fear and terrible pain go away. It wasn't the time to speak of our Heavenly Father who never abandons us. Those words would only ring hollow. So I held J in my arms and told him to let the feelings come and let the tears flow.

"I can't," he said.

And that's all he said.

Usually upbeat and always gregarious, J didn't say a word during the memorial service or the funeral. Though he is a religious rapper who is never at a loss for words, no words have passed from his mouth in two days. A kid who loves colorful, hip fashions from Japan, he has not worn anything but a black suit, a white shirt, and a plain black tie since we arrived in Memphis.

I have left him alone. I have done so because I realize that he has crawled into a space where, at least for now, he cannot be reached. He does not want to be reached. He does not want to deal with the excruciating confusion that has filled his head and is attacking his heart.

"I have lost a child myself," I tell the mourners, referring to my son Darryl, who was murdered in Oakland by a drug dealer. "When it happened, no human words could comfort me. No human being could comfort me. I sought silence, and it was only in silence that I was able to struggle with my faith. Yes, *struggle*. I asked God, *Why?* I wanted to know, had to know, couldn't live without answers. The grief cried out for explanation. But none came. All I heard the Lord say was, 'I am love.' 'I need more than love,' I complained. 'Love is everything,' came the answer. 'I can only be what I am. And I am love.' Still, I wasn't satisfied because the pain and the injustice only grew deeper. My desperation to get out of that state of depression grew deeper. I was lost in a sea of mourning. I wanted my child back—plain and simple. Nothing else mattered. If Christ brought back Lazarus, let Christ bring back my Darryl. Let Christ intervene on my behalf. Let Christ turn back the hands of time and give me my son. Let things be different. Let my child live! Please, dear God, why did You receive my son so early? Why didn't You let my child live?

"I cried myself to sleep for many months. I read my Bible. A few psalms and proverbs helped—but not much. Mourning is an agonizingly slow process. I tried to speed the process, but when I did, that only prolonged it. I sat with the pain. I felt it. I argued with God. I questioned. I fell back into despair. I woke up shaking with anger. I saw Darryl's demise in nightmare after nightmare. I went through whatever I went through.

"You will have to go through whatever you are going through. I can only stand before you as a grieving mother who still grieves. I can only say that I am here to affirm your right to question your faith and argue with your God. You do not need to deny your humanity. You do not need to pretend you are not feeling all the things you are feeling. God is great enough to absorb it all. He is the Great Listener and, I believe, through His divine listening, He is the Great Healer. But healing is not instantaneous and grief of this magnitude is not short-lived.

"For the rest of my life, I know I will live with the awful fact that my son died so young, and so violently. That fact will have no resolution. It may never make sense. His passing is rooted in mystery. He had no chance to grow into a man. His time on earth still seems criminally brief. His physical death was horrendous. And yet, I stand before you, testifying to one simple fact: For all the questioning of my faith, it was my faith that got me through. Faith in a God who isn't always clear and whose blessings aren't always comprehensible. Faith in a God who gives and forgives, who fills our lives with passion, pleasure, pain, joy, despair, wonder, doubt, and, yes, ultimately love.

"So we cherish our children. We cherish their memories and we cherish their gifts. We love so deeply we cannot describe that love. We mourn their loss so deeply that we cannot describe that mourning. So we stay silent, in dialogue with the God who created us all. We listen to the sound of the children singing out— and we say, thank You, Lord, thank you for life eternal. In Jesus' name, Amen."

The music is turned up louder and voices fill the small school auditorium. For the next five minutes, we sit in silence as the children's voices penetrate our hearts.

Shaleena's house in West Memphis is a one-story two-bedroom bungalow in immaculate condition. Shaleena was always the model of neatness. When she joined the Raelettes, she was very young. When she died last week, she was only thirty-eight. J is her only child. Shaleena and J were extremely close, the way single mothers and their children tend to be. Shaleena never married. After Julius, she was extremely cautious about entering into a relationship. There had been a few boyfriends over the years, but nothing serious. Shaleena was devoted to J and to her mission as a teacher of young children.

I'm thrilled to say that, shortly after J's birth, Shaleena found the Lord. Whenever in Los Angeles, she and J stayed with me and attended House of Trust, the old bank building on Adams Boulevard that my wonderful congregation converted to a church. Shaleena and I prayed together often; we called each other every week. She was my singing buddy, my kid sister, my dear friend. When J was born and I was asked to become his godmother, I thanked Shaleena for the privilege. When he was five, we all spent August in a rental house up the California coast near Oxnard. When J was seven, he stayed with me for two weeks while his mother completed her master's degree in music. He was always highly verbal, highly active. He loved language and talked before he walked. He loved life and he loved his mother. She was his closest friend and truest protector. When his talent for rapping blossomed and his mother suggested that he apply that talent to the Gospel of Jesus, he did just that. There were no arguments or conflicts. J was always a good boy—obedient, dutiful, eager to please his elders.

When it turned out that J's charismatic personality lit up the stage and intrigued young churchgoers, Shaleena didn't hesitate to let him venture beyond Memphis. He rapped in churches in Nashville, then Chicago, then Atlanta. I saw him at a megachurch in Los Angeles only three months ago. The place was packed with preteens and teens who acted as though he were Usher or Chris Brown.

After the show, I took J back to my house, where he spent the night. The next morning I made him breakfast and we sat down for a little talk. I could see that show business—even gospel show business—had him on a fast track. I gently warned him about the pitfalls of big money and big ego, especially for someone so young.

"Don't have to worry about me, Aunt Tina," he said, "'cause

the Lord has my back. The Lord gets my glory, and the Lord directs my path."

"I'm glad to hear that, baby, 'cause the world has a way of confusing all of us."

"It's all good, Aunt T, it's all moving the way it needs to move."

Now, in the house where he grew up, J isn't moving at all. I have never seen the boy in this condition. It's as though all his boundless energy has been drained from his young body. All vestiges of hope seem to be gone. He slouches, stares straight ahead.

I take his hand and ask him if he'd like to pray. His hand is limp, and he doesn't respond.

I stay silent. I realize that J doesn't want to hear the sound of my voice right now. He doesn't want to hear anything. He isn't ready, he isn't able to receive comfort. The boy is lost in despair.

Friends come by. Shaleena had many people who loved her. Local musicians. Her other students. The parents of the students. Her fellow teachers. The principal of her school. Her minister, her physician, J's physician, J's friends from all over the city, even some of J's fans.

When they greet him, all he can do is nod. When they tell him how sorry they are for his loss, his eyes barely blink. No one can engage him in conversation. Some try, but it's no use. J just sits there.

There is food and there is music. Someone plays the album that Ray Charles produced for the Raelettes when Shaleena and I were in the group. Then someone else plays the solo record that Shaleena released just after she left Ray. Her voice fills the room, and suddenly her warmth, her loving presence, and her sparkling personality flood our hearts.

As soon as the records start, as soon as J hears his mom's voice, he gets up and leaves. He doesn't emerge from his bedroom until two p.m. the next afternoon.

"Hungry, baby?" I ask him.

"Not very."

These are his first words.

I make him an omelet. He sees the morning newspaper, the Memphis *Commercial Appeal,* that's opened to a full-page obituary about his mother. There's a big picture of Shaleena leading the choral group, her hands extended in the air, an expression of joy on her face.

J looks away from the picture and studies his eggs. He takes a bite or two and then stares off into space.

I leave him alone the rest of the day. Mourning has its own life. Mourning takes as long as it takes. No one can rush it; no one can deny it; no one can make it go away. For J, this mourning process is not only incalculably deep, it is terribly new. No fifteen-year-old lives with the expectation of suddenly losing his young mother. There is no preparation for this. There is no getting ready, and there is no getting over it quickly. It is all new, the pain so fresh, the loss still unbelievable.

I decide to stay the week. My son, Andre, is calling and so is my daughter, Laura. They loved Shaleena and see J as their little brother. Justine is calling from Hawaii and my friend Mr. Mario is calling from Los Angeles. Everyone is concerned. Everyone is asking about J and wanting to speak to him on the phone. But he won't speak on the phone and, for the next forty-eight hours, he won't leave his room.

Now I'm worried. I think his depression has deepened to a critical level. He seems almost comatose. I don't know how to reach him, and I don't know what to do. I turn to God. That night I pray, *Father, show me, lead me, help me, strengthen me. Give me wisdom and give me insight. Let me reach this child with Your healing love. Let me comfort him with Your warmth. Let me show him Your Light. Let Your Light shine on his heart. Let Your heart heal his. In Jesus' name, Amen.*

The weekend arrives and J is still moping around the house, saying nothing.

Come Sunday morning I ask him if he wants to go to church with me. He says yes. I'm praying for a breakthrough. I'm saying, *Thank you, Jesus.* Shaleena's church is called the Way of the Healer. It's a nondenominational Bible-based Christian congregation. The minister is young, thirty or so, and excited to see J. All the young people are excited to see him. They are also sensitive to his loss and approach him with tenderness and consideration. There is no doubt, though, that his presence gives the church a lift. During the sermon the minister speaks of loss and its pain. He mentions Shaleena and praises her spirit, her dedication as a teacher, her devotion as a mom. He mentions J and asks him to step forward. He will not do so without me, so I accompany him to the front of the small sanctuary. We are then encircled by the entire congregation.

"In silence," the minister says with great sensitivity, "we pray for our young brother, for healing to come into his heart, for continuous love and understanding from his friends, for ongoing strength for his ministry."

The silence continues for several minutes. People are crying, some openly weeping. J is squeezing my hand. I feel him holding back tears. And then as each congregant, one by one, embraces him, he finally lets go. The tears flow. He weeps unashamedly. He releases his pain and fear, his confusion and panic, he releases it all. With each hug, his sobbing gets deeper and his tears flow freer.

"I'll still be afraid," he tells me that night.

"That's understandable, baby," I say.

"I'm afraid to be alone."

"I'm here with you."

"I think I'm afraid I can't . . . I can't even live without my mother. I don't think I can do that."

"You're doing it right now, sweetheart," I say.

"But this fear is all over me, Aunt T. I go to bed with the feeling, and I wake up with the feeling. I don't wanna go back to school. I don't wanna go back out there on the road now."

"There's no reason to, baby. The promoters will understand that you need this time off."

"But who will tell them? My mom handled all that."

"I'll tell them, baby. I'll tell them first thing tomorrow morning. You don't have to worry about it."

"And I'm afraid of living alone. I don't wanna live in this house alone."

"You won't be living alone."

"But my aunt can't take care of me. You know that. My aunt can't take care of herself. And my dad's brother, I don't even know him. I don't even know where he is. Somewhere in Detroit. I've only seen him a couple times in my life. I don't think he knows that Mama is gone."

"I've thought about this, honey, and I've prayed on it, and I feel the best thing would be for you to come to Los Angeles and live with me."

J lifts his head and looks at me. I can see the fear in his dark-brown eyes.

"You'd do that for me, Aunt Tina?"

"For you, for Shaleena, and for myself. You'd be a blessing in my life. I have an extra bedroom and, besides, my kids are grown with lives of their own. Having a young person around would do me a world of good. Especially when that young person is my one and only godson."

J gets up and embraces me.

"Thank you, Aunt T. Thank God for you."

"I thank God for you, baby."

MOTHERHOOD

ALL MY LIFE I called my mama "Mother Dear." She was a God-fearing woman who raised her children with the right mixture of divine love and worldly wisdom. She employed discipline. She believed in praising when we did well and spanking when we acted up. But what she did most of all was provide me with a model of what it meant to be a mother. Comes down to two words:

Children first.

Children before your own interests. Children before your own pleasure. Children before your comfort or satisfaction.

The kids come first. The kids need your time and the kids need your respect. The kids need your attention. The kids require your all.

Whatever the fancy books on child rearing may say, I never forgot that lesson: The babies are paramount.

I remember J as a baby, cute, curious, practically walking

before he crawled. Beautiful baby. I baptized him. I said, "May this boy become a loving servant of God."

He became that. He is that. And sitting next to him on the plane from Memphis to Los Angeles, I'm feeling gratitude for his presence in my life.

But I'm also feeling uncertainty.

I am no spring chicken. I am in my seventies. My energy is great and my health good. People tell me I look fifty-five, but motherhood is a job for young women. Motherhood is the most demanding job there is. It's physically draining and it's emotionally draining. When you do follow my own mother's rule—as you must—and give kids your all, the result is that there's not much left for you.

Am I ready to give J my all?

I am a full-time minister with a decent-sized congregation. My parishioners have many needs. Sunday there's church all day. Wednesday night is Bible class. There are hospital visitations two to four days a week. There are funerals. There are seminars. There are retreats. There are business meetings and planning committees.

Of course I've always been a working mom. I sang and was out on the road when my older children were young and I managed. I will manage with J. But when my kids were young I was young. J's a teenager and, for lack of a better word, I am a senior citizen. He's an MC and a rapper. Sure, it's Christian rap, and sure he's working in the church, but his way of invoking God's word is new and radically different from mine. There's also the fact that his mom, a much younger woman than myself, advised him and, in fact, managed him in the field of gospel entertainment. Sure, I used to be in show business, but that was a long time ago. Things have changed.

Then there is, I must confess, my own reluctance to give so

much of myself. I am, I confess, somewhat selfish. Having raised children, I feel like I've already done my job. Don't I deserve a break? I can't express these feelings to anyone except my friend Justine. I tell her this on the phone.

"Sure you deserve a break," she tells me, "and you don't have to feel guilty to say so. But I'll tell you something, Albertina, you're going to take care of that child anyway."

"What makes you so sure?" I ask.

"You've told him so. And you never break your promise. I've known you forever and I haven't seen you do it yet."

I sigh. Justine continues.

"But go ahead and keep telling me all the reasons it's going to be tough, because it is. I personally think you were a little crazy to make that promise, but that's Albertina. Fools walk in where angels fear to tread."

"You calling me a fool, Justine?"

"A fool and an angel both."

I sigh again.

"Listen here," says Justine, "at the very least your life will get a lot more interesting. And it may make you finally realize you need a man."

"Justine, please."

"Please, nothing. Every boy needs a father. And I think Mr. Mario would do just fine in that role. Have him move in and the three of you can play house."

"That's the other line, Justine, I gotta go."

"It's probably Mr. Mario himself. Time for his nightly booty call."

"All right, Justine, you've had your fun."

"I wish you'd have some fun, Albertina."

"I'm doing just fine, baby."

I switch lines and sure enough it is Mr. Mario.

"You're back," he says.

"I am. With the boy."

"Where is he?"

"Napping."

"How is he?"

"As well as can be expected, Mario. He's been through so much."

"And you intend to keep him?"

"I do."

"I'm glad."

"You are?" I ask.

"Of course I'm glad. You're a wonderful woman and a wonderful mother, not to mention a wonderful friend. I can't imagine you doing anything else *but* caring for the child."

"He's no child, Mario. He's a teenager. And in the gospel world, he's a teenage star."

"Is he talented, Albertina?"

"In the extreme."

"Cocky?"

"I don't think so. He loves the Lord."

"You can love the Lord and still be cocky," says Mario. "Is he into girls?"

"I'm not sure, but girls are sure into him."

"Is he sexually active?"

"Mario, his mama just died in a tragic accident. Do you think this is the time to ask him questions like that?"

"If not now, soon. Men tend to drown their sorrows in sex. I know that from experience."

"Oh do you?" I say in surprise.

"And because he's had no father, someone needs to talk to the boy."

"Are you volunteering?"

"Yes, Albertina, I am. The boy needs a father figure. I'm around all the time anyway. And he won't do any better than me."

"If you say so yourself," I say.

"I say that a woman needs a man to help raise a child. A woman can do it alone. And a man can do it alone. But a kid needs both. You wouldn't argue with that, would you, Albertina?"

"I would not."

"Then I'm staying around. I'm getting involved."

In my mind I wonder if Mario's attitude has more to do with me than with J, whom he barely knows. I wonder if this is Mario's way to get closer to me and prove his worth as a companion. I wonder many things but decide not to voice them—not now. Mario's fundamentally right. J has moved in, and I can use some help.

The Bishop Is Back.

Saturday afternoon. I'm seated in my living room reading the Bible and preparing tomorrow's sermon. I look out the window and immediately understand what is happening. I've seen this stretch limo before. I know who it belongs to, and I know exactly who's about to step out of the car. Bishop Henry Gold of the Fellowship of Faith in Dallas, Texas.

As usual, Bishop is immaculately dressed. His dark-blue suit is silk and custom tailored to his slender frame. The drape is quite perfect. Not a hair of his silver mane is out of place. His brown skin glows with good health. His teeth are even and straight. His gold-rimmed glasses carry the double "G" of the Gucci brand. As he walks toward my house, he speaks on a cell phone. As I open the door, he completes his call, puts his phone away, and reaches to shake my hand.

"Pastor Merci," he says, "it's always a blessing to see you."

"Good afternoon, Bishop," I say.

I can't say I'm happy to see him. He is, after all, the man who tried to take over my congregation with a megachurch right here in Los Angeles. God forgive me for judging, but it's hard not to when it comes to Bishop Gold. To my mind he teaches the gospel of prosperity, not the gospel of Christ. Christ promises us *spiritual* gains according to Matthew 6:33: "But seek first His kingdom and His righteousness, and all these things will be added to you." If we read the Good Book literally, as the good Bishop claims he does, we're to put down our pursuit of worldly goods to follow Jesus.

"Glad I found you at home, Pastor," he says. "I called earlier and spoke to J. He invited me to come by. I hope you don't mind."

"Of course not. He's in the back watching television. Let me tell him that you're here, Bishop."

Of course I know that J has performed at Gold's church, but beyond that I know nothing of their relationship. When I tell J that Bishop is here, he gets up at once to greet him.

I'm surprised to see J and Gold embrace.

"My son," says Bishop, "my heart has been with you ever since I heard the news. We've all been praying for you. We've all been weeping with you."

"Thank you, sir," says J, always a model of good manners.

"How have you been holding up, son?" asks Bishop.

"First week was rough, but my godmother here kept me from losing it. I came pretty close."

"Your godmother is a blessing to us all," says Bishop.

I say nothing. I know the man has no use for me, and I also know he's a hypocrite. But I believe in restraint of tongue—and I'm restraining like crazy.

"Will you be moving back to Memphis, son?" asks Bishop.

"I think I'll be living here with Aunt T," J answers.

"Wonderful," says Bishop. "But always remember that you have a home with us in Dallas. In fact, there's a whole wing of my new home that's unoccupied and waiting for you. It's unoccupied because Damitra has moved out here to live with my wife's sister."

"Damitra told me she wanted to live in L.A. and do her last year of high school where they had better music courses," says J.

"Well, whatever my daughter wants, my daughter seems to get," says Bishop. "She's one determined young woman. Matter of fact, she wanted to see you today and should be coming shortly."

"Great," says J.

"Can I offer you some tea or coffee, Bishop?" I ask. "Perhaps a slice of blueberry pie."

"Thank you, Pastor. Don't mind if I do."

I go to the kitchen to prepare the refreshments. When I return carrying a tray, Bishop and J are caught up in a serious conversation about plans for late August.

"I'm set to speak at six churches up and down the East Coast," Bishop explains, "and I'd like to take you and Damitra along. I want to reach the young people, and with your rapping and Damitra's singing I think I stand a far greater chance."

I am presuming that Damitra is a gospel singer. But since I have not been invited into the conversation, I am asking no questions. Just listening.

"I don't know if I'll be ready, Bishop," J says.

"Performing at those churches will do you a world of good. I'm certain that's what your mother would want."

I want to step in and say something. How does Gold know what his mother would want? Gold may have met Shaleena, but he sure didn't know her, certainly not like I did. J's mother would want calm and quietude for her son—that's what she would want. But rather than start an argument, I maintain my silence. I can always speak to J later, when we are alone.

"There's also the matter of management," says Gold. "It's something I had mentioned to your mom. She was quite interested in the fact that our church has a management division for musical artists. We represent their interests. We find their bookings and we negotiate their fees. Because we know the gospel market so intimately, we're able to ensure our artists work at the highest possible pay level."

This is how Bishop has chosen to conduct his condolence call? By bringing up business? By giving J a sales pitch for his management company? By God, this man is something else!

Still, I stay silent.

"That sounds good, Bishop, but right now my mind's not on that kind of stuff," says J.

Of course not, I think. Leave the boy alone! He's just lost his mother!

At that point the doorbell rings.

Standing there is Damitra Gold, a seventeen-year-old who, at least to me, looks like she is going on twenty-five. She is J's height, practically six feet tall. She is statuesque. Her clinging silver blouse and tight slim blue jeans display her figure quite dramatically. She has her father's deep brown fiery eyes and her father's gregarious nature.

"I'm Damitra," she says, offering her hand, heavy with several gold bracelets and a big dome sapphire ring. "You must be Pastor Merci."

"Pleasure to meet you," I say.

"I love your singing, Pastor. My folks have all your records. You are so blessed."

"Thank you, darling," I say. "Thank you very much."

Salutations out of the way, she makes a beeline for J and gives him a big hug that in my estimation lasts a little too long.

"I am so so sorry, J," she says. "I've been thinking about you night and day. I can't tell you how my heart goes out to you. I just thank God you have so many friends and fans who care so much about you."

"Thanks, Damitra," says J, who allows her to hold his hand.

"When I learned you were here in Los Angeles, I couldn't believe it. We're both living in the same city. Isn't that fabulous? My aunt's house is in Lafayette Square, only a few miles from here. We can write and rehearse together, J. We can be together whenever we want to."

The woman-child speaks in great torrents of emotion. Her personality is commanding and her energy high. She effortlessly takes over the conversation and, to my way of thinking, she seems to have taken over J. She very much follows her father's pattern of behavior. Because of J's psychological condition—he's still in the midst of mourning for his mother—I cannot detect whether he accepts the Golds' take-charge attitude or is simply too drained to argue. He and his mom always saw eye to eye. She endorsed his career and helped him in all ways, but she also made certain he stayed on top of his schoolwork. When he started rapping, J was only nine. His first performance came when he turned ten. Until this year, when J celebrated his fifteenth birthday, his mother Shaleena traveled with him on every out-of-town trip. Even when she let him perform in churches in Louisville or Detroit, she was careful that a responsible chaperone was with him at all times. Shaleena often discussed with me her concern about sexual precociousness among the young. "The last thing I want for J," she'd recently told me, "is to have his life complicated with an unwanted pregnancy."

"He seems so completely responsible," I replied, "that I don't think you have much to worry about." "I don't worry about J," Shaleena responded, "I worry about the girls around him. He has so many fans, and most of them are girls. Not all of them are as responsible as he is. He's at a vulnerable age. And no matter how much he loves the Lord, his hormones are kicking in. He's a healthy young man, and he's a physical young man. He can rap for two hours, he can go to the schoolyard and play basketball with the boys for another two hours, but he still has energy to spare. I worry, Albertina, I worry a lot."

Now I can't help but worry as I watch Damitra fall all over J. When she speaks to him, she acts as though her father and I aren't even in the room. She leans over and whispers in his ear. Her body language is loose and seems to be saying, "I'm available."

Or am I simply being too protective? Am I seeing things? Am I inventing a scenario that isn't there? This is a new season of motherhood for me, and I'm out of practice. God knows I am overprotective. This young man is now my responsibility. I confess to God that I have my prejudices. I don't like them, but they are there. I am prejudiced against Bishop Gold because I don't trust his motives and ambition. I am distrustful of his daughter because she does not dress or act her age. I am skeptical of how both Golds seem to be taking control of J's mind.

The visit is prolonged by Damitra's stories about her singing success. Her popularity as a performer who sings before her father delivers guest sermons around the country has grown. Now, she says, she's set to record her first solo gospel album. Damitra wants J to rap on the record. "You'll be the only featured guest artist," she says. "I want a picture of us on the cover."

The presumption is that J will do everything Bishop and his daughter ask of him. Mind you, they don't ask harshly. They certainly don't ask disrespectfully. They pay J compliment after compliment. They profess concern and love. To my mind, they overwhelm him with attention and the promise of all good things to come. They seem to raise his spirits and give him the impression that it is his welfare and his welfare only that concerns them. When they leave, there are embraces all around.

"May God bless you for bringing J to Los Angeles," says Bishop. "May God bless you and your wonderful congregation."

"Thank you," I say.

"If you don't mind, Pastor," says Damitra, "I'll be over often. You'll be my new aunt and I'll be your new niece."

"You couldn't ask for a more God-fearing protector," her father says.

As J and I look out the window we see Bishop get into his limo and Damitra slip behind the wheel of a white-on-white Mercedes. The top is down.

"Isn't she young to have a car of her own?" I ask J.

"She told me her father was able to get her a hardship license."

"Hardship?" I ask.

"She says it's hard for her to live without a car."

"What's a Picnic Without Frankie Beverly on the Box?"

Fourth of July, and Mario and I are throwing a back-yard picnic.

More accurately, I'm providing the backyard and Mario's providing the picnic. Mario owns Stay Out of the Kitchen, a health food café a few doors down from my church, House of Trust. A former TV actor and reformed lover of cheeseburgers and fatty pork, Mario turned over a new leaf last year. After the death of his wife from diabetes and a serious heart attack of his own, he saw the light that led him to clean living and healthy eating. His café, decorated with photos of all his fellow Hollywood actors—everyone from Robert Guillaume to John Amos to Cicely Tyson—serves a menu of low-fat meals prepared the right way: no trans fats, no dangerous oils, lots of fresh vegetables.

The picnic is a celebration of vegetables. Carrots, cucumbers, tomatoes, broccoli, string beans. There is a delicious dip, made from a mixture of mustard and lemon. There are veggie burgers sizzling on the grill, along with onions and red peppers. There are flourless chocolate cakes and soy ice cream in four different flavors. And there is, of course, Mr. Mario himself, all six feet two of him, wearing his white sky-high chef's hat and lording it over this whole affair. Mr. Mario is in his element.

My son, Andre, has flown in from Dallas and my daughter, Laura, is here from Chicago. My nephew Patrick, who serves as my assistant pastor, is also here with his wife, Rabbi Naomi Cohen, whose dad is black and mom is white. Blondie, my hairdresser and close friend for over forty years, is here along with twenty-five or thirty members of my congregation. Mixing among the crowd is my godson J, who is having a bad day. He woke up crying for his mother.

"It's a beautiful day," says my friend Barbara Vine, who has arrived with her fourteen-year-old granddaughter, Autumn. Autumn is a fresh-faced dark-skinned girl with a darling figure. Her peach tank top and white shorts reveal that she is physically quite mature.

"Is that J Love over there, Mommy?" I hear Autumn ask her grandma.

"Yes, dear," I tell the young girl. "He's my godson."

"Oh, my God!" Autumn exclaims. "That really *is* J Love!"

Autumn's eyes go wide.

"It's like when we first saw Sam Cooke," says Barbara. "Remember when he was singing with those Soul Stirrers, Albertina? Lord have mercy, that man was pretty."

"Would you like to meet J?" I ask Autumn.

"Yes, ma'am. Do you think I could get his autograph?"

"He'll be flattered," I say.

J's busy talking to my daughter, Laura, who, to my mind, looks a little thin. She's a hardworking schoolteacher who has devoted her life to helping inner-city kids. Laura has always had a huge heart and a tiny appetite.

"Y'all come meet Barbara and Autumn," I tell Laura and J.

They walk over to where we're standing next to the big oak tree. We make the proper introductions. Laura is wearing pink pedal pushers, a throwback to the fifties, and J is decked out in a pair of top-to-bottom camouflage shorts that match his camouflage hoody.

"Aren't you a little hot in that outfit, sweetheart?" I ask him.

"I love your outfit," says Autumn, looking up at J. "Isn't that A Bathing Ape?"

"What in the world is a 'bathing ape'?" asks Autumn's grandma.

"It's a Japanese clothing line," Autumn says. "It's the coolest. It's the company that gave Pharrell Williams all his clothing ideas."

"I'm afraid I don't know who Pharrell Williams is," I confess.

"Big-time hip-hop producer," says J.

"Does he produce gospel?" I ask.

"Not yet. But he's talked about producing me." J speaks glumly, with little enthusiasm.

"Have you met Chris Brown?" Autumn asks J.

"I've met him," says J.

"He's cool, isn't he?" Autumn inquires.

"He's okay," J assures her.

"I like your T-shirt," says Autumn.

J's white T-shirt, a double extra large that hangs on his long thin frame, has a pattern of crosses and hearts that spell out a large "J."

Autumn wants to know if J will be performing in Los Angeles anytime in the near future. J isn't sure. As he speaks, I can't help but feel the extreme sadness that sits in the depths of his soul.

Meanwhile, Autumn's grandmother is growing a little uneasy. I think Barbara is worried that Autumn is star struck and too forward with her questions. Of course I understand this. Mothers and grandmothers can't help but worry about their daughters—especially in this day and age when young girls of fourteen dress and sometimes act like women of twenty-one. I want to tell Barbara that she has nothing to fear from my godson, who's a perfect gentleman, but this is hardly the time.

Besides, Naomi and Patrick have come over to join us. In between bites of veggie burgers, they make friendly conversation. Naomi is especially friendly.

"I've heard so much about you, J," she says. "I'd love for you to come over and perform for my congregation."

"Do you work with my godmother at the House of Trust?" he asks.

"I do work with her," says Naomi. "We've done many programs together, but my congregation is Jewish. I'm a rabbi."

J looks confused.

"Isn't Patrick a preacher?" he asks.

"I sure am," says my nephew.

"And a Christian?" J asks. I see him making the effort to engage in conversation, and I'm glad.

"A blood-washed Christian," Patrick is quick to answer.

"So how does that work?" J wants to know.

"Wonderfully well," says Naomi.

"So far . . . " Patrick adds with a smile.

"Your church wouldn't mind me rapping about Jesus?" J asks Naomi.

"I think they'd be fascinated. I know I would."

"There's a Jewish rapper," says J. "An orthodox reggae rapper."

"Sure," says Naomi. "Matisyahu. I love his records."

"You listen to hip-hop?" asks J.

"Patrick knows more about it than I do. Patrick has a whole library of hip-hop records and books. He's a scholar on the subject."

"A fan," says Patrick, correcting his wife. "I saw Grandmaster Flash and the Furious Five when I was very young, and that hooked me for life. I wish there were hip-hop artists active in the church. That's why I'm so happy that you're doing your thing for the Lord, J. We need more J's running around here and making their beats."

"Amen," I say.

"I say it's time to stop the idle chatter and eat some of this organic corn," shouts Mr. Mario from across the yard. "You guys won't taste anything sweeter."

We walk over to the grill. Autumn stays behind with J. There is no way she is letting him out of her sight. She continues to pepper him with questions about his career. He's making an effort, but his eyes are still terribly sad.

Blondie is asking Mario if he plans to grill chicken.

"This is a birdless Fourth," says Mario. "We're letting our fine feathered friends fly free this holiday. Where's our star? Where's J? Let's get him over and hear some of that freestyle the rappers are famous for. What do you say, J?"

"You calling me out?" J asks.

"Time to rap for your dinner, son," says Mario, who has told me that he thinks the boy needs encouragement to perform. According to Mario, once a performer always a performer. And the way for a performer to beat back the blues is to get out there and wow an audience.

"I'd rather not," says J. "Not today."

"You're pushing the boy too hard," I whisper in Mario's ear. "Just let him be."

"What's a picnic without Frankie Beverly on the box?" asks Laura, who grew up on old-school rhythm and blues.

She puts on "Joy and Pain" and some folks start to dance.

"J isn't his old self, is he, Mama?" asks my son, Andre, who himself went through a difficult patch when he and his wife broke up. He works in Dallas, where he teaches creative writing in a private school and writes screenplays. He's had two scripts optioned by major producers and, I'm certain, will soon find success.

"When you lose a mama," I say, "it takes a long, long time. It takes forever."

"I don't even want to think about it. I wish there were something I could do to help him."

"You love him, son. Let him know that. That's a lot."

"I've asked him to go to the movies or just for a ride, but he seems tied to your house."

"He won't let me out of his sight," I say.

"He lost one mother," says Andre, "and he's afraid of losing another."

Stay out of the Kitchen

IT'S JUST WHAT HE NEEDS," says Mario.

"I'm not sure," I say.

"I am."

"You're always sure of yourself, Mario. That's your way."

"Hard work is always the way. Hard work is the only antidote to depression I know."

"What about God?" I ask.

"I've been trying God and God doesn't seem to be working."

"You're impatient, Mario," I say.

"I'm practical. The boy needs to get out of your house and do something. He's never had a man in his life who's told him what to do. I think it's about time."

It is early August and his mother has been gone two months. In spite of a few good days, J has sunk down into a deeper funk. My attitude is to give him more time, allow him the space to mourn and the sympathy that mourners require.

"Albertina, you're spoiling and indulging the boy," says Mario. "Time to get him off his behind. Nothing like good old-fashioned manual labor to get your mind off yourself."

"What do you have in mind?"

"He can work as a dishwasher. If he does that well, I'll promote him to busboy. And if he doesn't mess up, I'll show him the right way to cut up vegetables."

"And if he isn't interested in washing dishes or chopping veggies?"

"Tough. Life is tough. Better to learn that now than later."

"He already knows that, Mario. He lost his mother."

"He needs to go on, Albertina. He needs to get back in the real world. Moping around the house all day feeling sorry for himself is the worst thing for him. If you want to help him, enforce some regulations. Create some boundaries. Make him self-sufficient. He'll thank you for it later."

"But he's an artist."

"So am I, and so are you," says Mario. "But that doesn't mean we don't wash dishes. Gandhi said, 'Everyone needs to clean the latrines.' And he was the first to do so. So it's time we all follow Gandhi's lead. I'm telling you, Albertina, it's time to stop letting that boy sleep till two in the afternoon. Time to get the kid moving. Lay down the law. Be a good parent. Get tough."

I t takes me a week, but I see something must be done. J's moping around the house has to stop.

Autumn has been calling three or four times a day. She often stops by the house uninvited. She and J sit on the living room couch and listen to music or watch television. He is, of course, forbidden to bring her back to his bedroom, which seems to bother Autumn more than J. During her visits, he is polite with her, but he is mainly quiet and simply allows her to chat.

Damitra also visits and, from my vantage point, is even more of a temptress. Her outfits are far more revealing than Autumn's. To be blunt, Damitra has far more to reveal. One day she convinces J to take a ride in her sports car. When they leave at five p.m., I tell them that J's curfew is nine p.m., but they're back by six. I'm happy to see that J seems uninterested in Damitra's advances.

"Do you think J is gay?" asks Andre when I describe his indifference to these two girls.

"He's always liked girls," I say. "He's always had lots of girlfriends."

"He seems straight to me," says Andre. "I just think he's still messed up over his mama."

"I never knew a boy so extroverted in my life," I say. "I worry that all his high energy and bubbly personality have vanished."

"They'll be back," Andre assures me. "He just needs to get out of the house more."

"That's what Mario says."

"Mr. Mario's right."

Mario is waiting for J, apron in hand.

I've driven J over to Stay Out of the Kitchen at seven a.m. on a Monday morning.

When I told J last week that I wanted him to start working, he grunted and groaned. Then he saw I was serious and giving him no choice.

"As long as it's here in L.A.," he said. "And as long as I don't have any tour dates. I want to keep living at your house, Aunt T."

"It's not my house, J," I said. "It's *our* house. You are a permanent resident."

I explained that he needed something to take his mind off the past. I also said that Mario, given his upbeat nature, was a good guy to be around. But when I mentioned the word "dishwashing," J rolled his eyes.

I understood. What teenage boy wants to wash dishes?

When we get to the café, though, and J hears that Mario is blasting old-school R&B on the boom box, J's mood improves. His mama raised him on old school. Those sounds comfort him.

"Leave the boy to me," says Mario. "I'll bring him back to your place at the end of the day."

When J arrives home, he's exhausted.

"How'd it go?" I ask him.

"Mr. Mario's a good guy, but he's a slave driver. He's got me doing dishes, mopping the floor, and washing windows."

"Well, what doesn't kill you makes you stronger."

"I'm taking a hot bath, Aunt T."

"Good idea, baby."

While J's soaking in the tub, Mario calls.

"The program's working," he says. "The kid hung in there like a champ."

"He's a good boy."

"Little lazy around the edges, but responds well to discipline. By the end of the week he'll be the top dishwasher in the city."

"I'm not sure that's one of his goals," I say.

"But let me ask you this, Albertina: was he depressed when he got home?"

"No, just tired."

"And that's just the point. Physical labor can lessen emotional pain."

"Long as he's willing," I say.

"He's got no choice. You gave him no choice. That's why it's working."

I t works all week.

J gets there at seven a.m. and puts in a hard day's work. By the end of the week, Mr. Mario is teaching him to flip veggie burgers. J isn't jumping for joy, but he isn't complaining. He wants to please me and he knows he's doing so by helping out at Stay Out of the Kitchen.

"You ought to see the flock of young girls who are coming by to see him," says Mario. "Word's out, and they're lining up at the counter to get a stool so they can watch him make multi-grain flapjacks. He's pretty good at it too."

"Thank you for doing this, Mario. You're a true friend."

"You're more than a friend to me, Albertina. I've been telling you that for a long time. We're a pretty good couple when it comes to handling this kid. You're a righteous mom and my daddy skills are kicking in. I think J's on his way back from the dark side of the moon."

Week two starts out well. J likes the cooking more than the cleaning, and is proud to see that he can make whole-wheat French toast.

"Sounds like you're having fun, J," I say.

"Well, it sure isn't boring because your boyfriend doesn't stop talking."

"He's not exactly my boyfriend, J."

"He talks like he's your boyfriend. So who is he?"

"A good buddy."

That conversation takes place on Monday. On Tuesday J tells me he has to quit the job at the café.

39

"Why, baby?"

"Damitra got me a better job at a Christian bookstore that her father owns."

"What will you be doing there?"

"Nothing," he says. "Just sitting around."

"Why would they pay you to sit around and do nothing?"

"They sell my CDs and think I'll attract customers."

"Sounds boring, honey."

"If I don't have to do anything and I'm paid anyway, how can I argue?"

"Well, won't you be selling books and records?"

"Maybe, I'm not sure. But I think they just want me to hang out there."

"I'm not sure that's a good idea," I say.

"Why not, Aunt T? It's a Christian store. They only sell Christian merchandise."

"Well, if someone pays you, you need to work for that pay," I say.

"Shouldn't I just try it, though, for a day or two? What's to lose?"

"How about Mr. Mario? He's depending on you."

"He has other people helping him. He doesn't really need me. He just had me working there because of you."

"I don't know, J."

"Please, Aunt T."

J says it so sweetly I'm hard-pressed to refuse him. So I don't.

You don't know what you're doing, Albertina," says Mario, who comes over to the house that night. J is in his bedroom watching the Lakers.

"I'd have to agree with you," I say. "When it comes to teenagers, I'm out of shape."

"Teenagers are manipulators. The boy's manipulating you."

"The boy has a better job."

"The boy has a nothing job. They're paying him to sit around on his butt and flirt with girls."

"You know a teenage boy who'd refuse a job like that? What would you have done when you were his age, Mario?"

"That's not the point."

"That *is* the point. He showed he could work hard if we insisted."

"For a few days . . ."

"But then he came up with something better."

"His girlfriend's daddy came up with something better."

"She's not his girlfriend."

"Bishop Gold sure is her daddy! And Bishop Gold is the most controlling man I know."

"Bishop Gold is in Dallas."

"Which is where J will wind up if you keep giving him free rein. I'm telling you, Albertina, you gotta take hold of this situation before it takes hold of you."

That evening at about eleven o'clock the situation grows more complex.

Mario has gone home. I've gone to bed. I've closed my Bible, closed my eyes, and am drifting off to sleep when I hear a noise at the back of the house by J's room. I grow concerned. The windows to my house have no bars. I've never wanted my home to look like a prison. I have locks on the windows but during the summer the windows are usually left open so a breeze can blow through the screens. Anyone who wants to could easily remove a screen and climb through. I think what I'm hearing is just that—someone removing a screen. Alarmed, I get out of bed, throw on a robe, and hurry to J's room. When I open his door, I see Autumn coming through the window. I sigh.

J is naked except for a pair of baggy basketball shorts. Autumn is wearing short shorts and a tight halter top.

All of us remain speechless.

"I didn't know she was coming here," J says to me quickly. "I didn't invite her."

"It's my fault, Reverend Merci," says Autumn.

I still don't say anything.

"Will you have to tell my grandmother?" asks Autumn.

"Where does your grandmother think you are?" I ask.

"Asleep."

"You snuck out of the house?"

"I just wanted to spend some time with J. Please don't tell my grandmother."

"I'm afraid I'm going to have to, child. I'm going to have to call her right now. If she wakes up and finds you missing, she'll be worried to death."

I identify with Autumn's grandmother because she is raising the child alone. Autumn's mom died of a drug overdose when Autumn was an infant. My friend Barbara Vine stepped in and saved the child's life.

When I explain the situation to Barbara, she is, as I expected she'd be, irate.

"I'm coming over there right now to get her."

When she arrives, we are all sitting in the living room. J has put on a T-shirt.

As soon as she walks through the door, Barbara comes over and slaps Autumn across her face. It's a vicious slap. Autumn's skin turns scarlet and she bursts into tears.

"It's my fault, Mrs. Vine," says J. "I invited her here."

"I thought you said you hadn't invited her," I say.

"I was being nice. I was trying to protect her," says J.

Now I'm confused. Barbara Vine is not.

"They're both liars," she says. "It doesn't matter who says what. I just want to know if they've had unprotected sex."

"No, ma'am," J is quick to say.

"I want the truth, Autumn," Barbara demands. "The truth."

"We've kissed," she admits. "We've fooled around."

"I want the details of the fooling around," Barbara insists.

"Not all-the-way fooling around."

"I don't believe you," says Barbara.

"She's telling the truth, Mrs. Vine," says J.

"I don't believe *you* either," Barbara states. "I want you both to have an HIV test, first thing tomorrow morning."

Barbara is a registered nurse and, when it comes to health, she's serious business.

"But that's a waste of time, Mrs. Vine," J pleads. "There's nothing to be tested for."

"There's *everything* to be tested for. And unless your god-mother objects, I'm making sure you both get tested."

How can I object?

They are two teenagers. Obviously and understandably they are attracted to each other.

Am I to believe J that nothing serious has happened when, only a minute ago, I caught him in a lie?

What am I to believe?

Only that a test makes sense.

Please, Aunt T, don't make me go for that test," says J when Barbara has taken Autumn home, after having told her that she is grounded for two months.

"I feel like it's the responsible thing to do, sweetheart."

"But I swear, I haven't had sex with Autumn."

"May I ask you a very personal question, J?"

"Okay."

"Have you had sexual intercourse with a woman?"

"Well, I'm not exactly sure."

"J, how in the world can you *not* be sure about something like that? You either have or you haven't."

"Well, I think I was a little tipsy."

"You were drunk?"

"Not really drunk, tipsy, and we were fooling around, and I think it got pretty serious but I'm not sure."

"Who was the girl?"

"Damitra."

"Damitra Gold?"

"But it wasn't her fault, Aunt T. Wasn't really anyone's fault. We were at this party given by the kids in the choir. There was this punch, and someone had spiked it, but we didn't know that. Damitra and I kept drinking the punch 'cause it was sweet and it was making us feel good."

"Where did this happen?"

"In Dallas. It was at a big party given by Damitra's friends. We were all having a great time and somehow Damitra and I wound up in an empty bedroom where we started dancing and fooling around and next thing I know Damitra and I are in the bed together."

I shake my head in wonder.

"So you may well have had sex," I say.

"Maybe," says J, "but maybe not. I was a little drunk and my memory kinda washed away."

"Well, were you wearing protection?"

"I don't think so."

"J," I say, "what is Damitra's memory of this episode?"

"All she said is that we had fun."

"Has she been tested?"

"I wouldn't ask her something like that."

"And did you mention any of this to your mom?"

"Not really."

"What do you think she would have said?"

"She would have whopped my butt."

"Yes, she would have."

I stop to think. There's not much I can say. What's done is done.

"How long ago did this happen?" I ask.

"Sometime last year."

"So we're certain that Damitra isn't pregnant."

"You saw her yourself, Aunt T. She's thin as a pencil."

"And certainly her father knows none of this."

"He'd kill her. He'd kill us both."

"And have there been other girls, J?"

"Girls that did things to me, but I didn't do anything to them."

"What girls are these?" I ask.

"Girls who'd come back to the dressing room after a concert."

"And exactly what would happen?"

"Well, they were interested in pleasing me . . . you know . . ."

"Orally?"

"I guess that's the nice word."

"And that's all that was involved?"

"I promise, nothing more, I didn't even have to touch them."

"And that didn't make you feel bad for them, J?"

"They offered, Aunt T. It's something they wanted to do. Something they were dying to do."

"Without even knowing you . . ."

"They knew my music. They liked my rapping."

"The music that gave the glory to God. And the God who says that in order to respect Him we must respect ourselves. Do you think these girls respected themselves, J?"

"I can't answer that question, Aunt T. We didn't talk very much."

"And where was your mother when all this was happening? I know Shaleena would never have approved of this."

"Well, when she came to my concerts none of this did happen. She wouldn't allow those girls in the dressing room. But she couldn't attend every concert, and I could pretty easily lose the chaperones she hired."

I heave another long sigh and look deep into J's eyes. He is a sweet young man who doesn't want to hurt a soul. He's been deeply hurt by his mother's death. He is the object of adulation by young women who find him irresistible. He is part of a culture for whom promiscuity at a frighteningly young age has become a way of life.

And now he has become my responsibility.

"Look, J," I say, "it's clear that you have a fair amount of sexual experience. Given that fact, testing is not only an intelligent move, it's also mandatory. I'll arrange it all tomorrow morning."

"There's no way I can get out of it, Aunt T?"

"No," I reiterate. "No way in the world."

I toss and turn the rest of the night. My mind can't rest, my thoughts stumble over each other.

I think about young people. I think about the days when I

was young. I married young. I married three times. Back then, before I was saved, I was not inexperienced when it came to physical relationships, and I enjoyed myself. At a very young age, I understood that boys were made to hunt and girls were the game. But I also remember the Smokey Robinson song that says, "When the Hunter Gets Captured by the Game." Now young girls had become hunters. Could I blame J for not resisting their advances? I remember that before Shaleena found God, she also had her trying time with men. There had been more than a few in her life. She raised J without a husband. No righteous man was around to give him guidance, but J grew up to be an exceptionally sweet young man. I can see why girls like him. But climbing through his bedroom window—isn't that taking it awfully far? And taking him to an unsupervised party with spiked punch and empty bedrooms—isn't that what Damitra did?

I am no prude. I lived the rhythm and blues life for many years. I didn't drink and I didn't drug and I was certainly never out of control when it came to men. But I did see firsthand what celebrity can do. Celebrity changes the chemistry and alters the dynamics. Everyone is intoxicated by celebrity. And when it comes to male stars, females easily lose it. I saw women who were normally perfectly behaved go wild. I saw them lose the last vestiges of self-respect, restraint, and acceptable behavior. So why am I shocked by the actions of Autumn and Damitra?

Because they are so young. Autumn is fourteen, a year younger than J. Damitra is seventeen, two years older. They are adolescents whose precocious sexual behavior is nothing short of alarming. But at least these are girls who know him. But what about the others he mentioned, the girls who are willing to please him backstage as simply anonymous fans? How old are they? Thirteen? Twelve? I shudder to think about it.

But wait a minute. How old were my friends Mary Wilson, Florence Ballard, and Diana Ross when they formed the Primettes, the group that eventually became the Supremes? Fifteen years old. J's age. How old was Stevie Wonder when he was discovered by Ron White of the Miracles? Eleven. Or Michael Jackson when he and his brothers were discovered by Bobby Taylor? Ten.

And when I went out on the road as a background singer with James Brown and Bobby Bland and Wilson Pickett, wasn't I myself still in my teens? And didn't I see dozens of girls, not yet women, become pregnant by entertainers they barely knew? Wasn't it as promiscuous back then as it is now?

As I toss and turn, I keep thinking. I keep saying to myself that this is different because this is the world of gospel. These are young people serving God who should be responding to J's sacred raps. He is not telling them to lose their scruples, he is not seducing them, he is giving them God's word. That's different than the secular world of hyped-up hip-hop. Or at least it's supposed to be. But when I think about it even more, I remember that when Sam Cooke was still singing with the Soul Stirrers, the great gospel group, before he went pop, women threw themselves as wildly at him—perhaps even more wildly—than when he left the church to sing for the world. I remember his walking down the aisle of C. L. Franklin's New Bethel Baptist sanctuary in Detroit singing "Touch the Hem of His Garment" with women reaching out to touch the coat of his lime-green suit. I remember how Mahalia Jackson once told me, "Honey, if you think the jazz men have wild parties, you should see what's happening when the saints stop praying and get to playing."

I remember that it's always difficult to stay sane in the world of stars. Stars overstimulate our senses. Stars can drive you—as well as themselves—absolutely crazy.

Right now I'm feeling a little crazy because I realize I may have taken on more than I can handle. I am suddenly in the middle of the life of not merely an average teenaged boy—that would be difficult enough—but a teenager who is also a star. Making matters even more complex, that star has lost his mom, and perhaps his bearings. But maybe he lost his way even before Shaleena's terrible accident. With so many girls coming at him from every direction, perhaps he lost his bearings without his mother ever knowing.

Whatever the case may be, he is now my son. He is now my sacred responsibility. And like it or not, I must enter the fray.

Help me, dear Lord, I pray, *as I navigate unchartered waters. Help me find my direction. Help me through my confusion. Help me lead this boy to where You are. Help me keep You in him, as You stay in me, as You stay in all of us: a forever friend, a constant companion, a beacon, a force, a protector, a savior of our souls. In Jesus' holy name, Amen.*

COMING HOME

"HERE ARE MORE THINGS in heaven and earth, Horatio, than are dreamt of in your philosophy," says Mr. Mario, quoting Shakespeare.

"Hamlet is speaking to his friend Horatio," he explains. "He's describing what cannot be explained. We are now attending an event about which I must say the same."

Mr. Mario is dressed in a beautiful blue pin-striped suit. J's suit is white linen. I'm wearing my favorite silk skirt and matching silk blouse, both in a goldish orange. The House of Trust is packed, and the atmosphere is celebratory. I can feel the joy.

Today it is my supreme privilege to baptize Rabbi Naomi Cohen in the name of the Father, the Son, and the Holy Ghost.

This is a blessing on more levels than a mere mortal like me can understand.

First, the fact that I officiated at the marriage of Naomi and my nephew Patrick was a great blessing. Their romantic reconciliation, after a series of seemingly insurmountable challenges, was absolutely wonderful.

"You may have married them," Mario told me at the time, "but you'll never convert her."

"I'm not trying to convert her," I said. "I'm not trying to convert anybody."

"I thought you're mandated to convert everybody," Mario speculated.

"I'm mandated to follow God's will. But it's God who changes hearts, it's God who converts darkness into lightness. If I can reflect that lightness, I give the glory back to God."

Now, many months later, God will get the glory for this blessing that is compounded not only by Rabbi Cohen's baptism but by the baptism of a dozen members of her congregation. Understandably, her congregation experienced a shock when she announced her acceptance of Christ. But she did so with such empathy and understanding that even those members who did not follow her wished her well. I was at Temple Abraham during the Saturday service when she said, "There is one God, and there is one reality. I believe God is that reality. I also believe Christ was the manifestation of that reality on earth. I believe His death is our life, and that, as the second Adam, He carried His Father's faith. He was—He is—His Father's faith. He and His Father are one, just as we all are one in His redemptive power. For me, this is an idea that I've resisted for some time, but God has created circumstances in my life that have melted that resistance. I do not want to argue or try to convince any of you that I am right. But only that I am changed, and the result of that change—if it is, as I believe it to be, a true change—will be my ability to give and receive more love, love from God, love directed to each of you. Christ is about nothing but love, Christ is the highest expression of love, Christ is the very reality of love. In that sense, I am loving this change in my life and praying that love, in every positive form, will wash over this congregation as never before."

The congregation of Temple Abraham found a new rabbi, a young man from Hartford, Connecticut, but their feelings for Naomi were so overwhelmingly loving that they gave her a beautiful dinner—and invited both Patrick and me! Never had I seen a transition from one faith to another go so smoothly.

"That's because it's all one faith," Naomi explained. "We express it differently, but underneath the words is the strength of a loving, compassionate, forgiving God."

That God is surely manifest today in the House of Trust. The candidates for baptism are wearing white robes and seated in the first row. Behind them are members not only of my congregation, but Naomi's former congregation as well. Sensing her sincerity, they have to see her rebirth.

I love baptism. I love the ritual. I love the font, the deep immersion, the symbolism of reemergence, of going from the depths to the heights, of reenacting Christ's own baptism, of the echo of the Father's voice saying that He is well pleased, of the purging, the cleansing, the freshness, the newness, the joy, the devotion to a God who perfectly loves all of us, with all our imperfections.

My sermon is short.

I explain what has happened. "When my nephew Patrick began to date Naomi, many of you remember that there was much talk about what would happen. Patrick loves the Lord—I don't have to tell you that. But I did have to remind him that nothing is more off-putting than insensitive proselytizing. I pointed out that no one does the work of bringing people to God better than God. But when it comes to bringing people to Christ, we are understandably impatient. Christ is not. We are overly eager. Christ is not. We are insistent, even dogmatic. Christ is not. Christ isn't going anywhere. He was here before and He'll be here after. When we see His reality, we understand that until then our vision has been limited. When we embrace Him, our vision is expanded all the way to glory. The fact that so many wonderful people in this very church today have decided to embrace Him is testament to His infinite patience.

The high point, of course, is the act itself, the holy rite of immersion in the cleansing water. When I take Naomi by the hand and bring her to the font, I experience a moment of exquisite serenity. I see serenity in her eyes. As she closes her eyes and goes under, I pray fervently, just as I pray for all of those who have come from her congregation to accept Christ as the Son of the living God.

When she emerges from the font, her eyes are smiling, with an expression of exquisite clarity. There are shouts of praise and cries of jubilation. I glance at Mario, seated on the front row. Are there tears running down his cheeks or is that just my imagination?

After the celebration, Naomi is aglow with goodwill. "Feels like I've come home," she says.

She and Patrick are holding hands. My nephew is strangely silent. Usually talkative and quick to analyze, on this day he is awestruck by the enormity of the event. He is content to listen to his wife, stand by her side and enjoy the beauty of the moment.

"What are your plans now?" Mr. Mario asks Naomi.

"I've been accepted into a program for a Doctorate of Philosophy in Religion. Meanwhile, with Albertina being as busy as she is now that she has J, I hope to help out at House of Trust along with Patrick."

"Another great blessing," I say.

"And how about you, Mr. Mario," asks Naomi. "Has Albertina been successfully chipping away at that armor that protects your heart?"

"I'll grant you that Albertina's pretty strong, but so is my armor."

We all laugh.

Naomi, filled with the ever-new spirit of the Lord, goes on to say, "I'm not sure that armor of yours has much of a chance against God."

"Old doubters die hard," he says.

"But no one wants to die alone," Patrick adds.

"Or without their convictions," Mario remarks.

"Convictions change," says Naomi. "You saw change today. Amazing and miraculous change."

What follows is a strange and long silence among us all.

Finally, Mario says, "According to the English poet Alfred Lord Tennyson, 'There lives more faith in honest doubt than in half the creeds.'"

"And in that regard," I can't help but add, "my lovely friend Mario is the most honest of men."

The Jazz Bakery

T my age it feels strange to say that I'm dating. Well, I am. I'm dating Mario, and I'm happy. I'm happy because he's intelligent, he's fascinating, and, what's more, our cultural interests are much the same. Take tonight, for instance.

Tonight Mario and I are seated next to each other in the Jazz Bakery, a large photographer's studio that's been converted into a small auditorium. The auditorium sits inside a building that once housed a bread plant. It's all about transformation. The featured artist is my friend David Fathead Newman, who is transforming the old blues ballad "Willow Weep for Me" into a new song. His improvisations, lyrical and wildly romantic, virtually reinvent the song. David cries through his tenor sax, but his is not a cry of despair; his is a cry of love, a cry that transforms pain into beauty. He does the same with the song that made him famous, "Hard Times." When he plays "You've Changed," I hear the unsung lyrics inside every note. His reading of "Angel Eyes" takes my breath away. And in the end, when he switches to alto sax to explore the heart of "Misty," I turn to Mario, who has held my hand during the entire performance, and see a tear in the corner of his eye.

Afterward, we have dinner in a nearby French café.

"Beautiful concert," I say. "Thank you for taking me."

"Thank you for accepting my invitation. I know how busy you are."

"Never too busy for good music."

"And the wonder of it all is this: the older the jazz musician, the deeper his understanding of the poetry of his art."

"Age has its advantages," I say.

"The attainment of wisdom, musical or otherwise, is a life-time's work."

"The young certainly lack it."

"Thinking of J?" asks Mario.

"Hard not to. I'm still waiting for the results of his tests. And we leave next week for his concert in Dallas."

"That's next week," Mario reminds me. "We're here tonight, so let's enjoy ourselves."

"You're right to remind me, Mario. God wants us rooted in the now. God is present tense. He's present."

"He certainly seemed present at Naomi's baptism."

"Am I hearing right!" I exclaim. "Are you, my dear, actually admitting to the presence of God?"

"If you call Him a spirit of love, I am."

"He is *the* spirit of love."

"Well, then, let love ring out."

The waiter sets down our salads. I take Mario's hand and say, "Thank you, Father, for this food and the food of eternal love. In Jesus' name we say Amen."

"Amen," says Mario.

I take a bite of crisp lettuce and begin to reflect. "Been quite a summer."

"'Thy eternal summer shall not fade,'" says Mario.

"Shakespeare?"

"Yes, indeed. A line from one of his most famous sonnets."

"Would you like to recite it?"

"You know I would," says Mario. And he does:

> Shall I compare thee to a summer's day?
> Thou art more lovely and more temperate:
> Rough winds do shake the darling buds of May,
> And summer's lease hath all too short a date:
> Sometime too hot the eye of heaven shines,
> And often is his gold complexion dimmed,
> And every fair from fair sometime declines,
> By chance, or nature's changing course untrimmed:
> But thy eternal summer shall not fade,
> Nor lose possession of that fair thou ow'st,
> Nor shall death brag thou wand'rest in his shade,
> When in eternal lines to time thou grow'st,
> So long as men can breathe or eyes can see,
> So long lives this, and this gives life to thee.

"That was beautiful, Mario," I say.

"That's because it's written beautifully."

"And because you feel it so deeply."

He takes my hand and gently brings it to his lips.

I close my eyes and smile.

After a delicious meal and two hours of good conversation, Mario drives me home. David Newman's latest CD is coming through the speakers. The song is "It's That Ole Devil Called Love Again." But tonight love is no devil. Love is a light; love is the moonlight that shines down on us as we head for home; love is David's sax clearing the path, leading us to the safety of fellowship and faith in the goodness of true friendship.

Mario walks me to the door, kisses me on the cheek, and makes sure I'm safely inside.

J is up, sitting on the living room couch watching television. He smiles when he sees me.

"Finally!" he says in jest. "Now I can go to bed and not worry about you being out all night."

I laugh and greet him with a hug. "I appreciate your concern," I say.

"Someone's got to watch over Aunt T. Might as well be me."

"You're in a good mood."

"Got good news earlier. The HIV test came back clean."

"And Autumn?" I ask.

"Her test was also negative."

"Praise God!"

"Gotta say I'm relieved, Aunt T."

"And you called the girls to tell them?"

"Sure did."

"Wonderful. Shall we give thanks to God?"

"Always."

"Father," I say, "we thank You for all our blessings, especially the gift of good health. With strong body and clear mind, may we serve You with even greater dedication. May we give You the glory! In Jesus' name, Amen."

"Amen," J echoes.

"What's on TV?"

"This really interesting documentary on PBS about singers who left the church for pop."

58

"That's about everybody."

"And everybody's in it—Little Richard, Ray Charles, Sam Cooke, Marvin Gaye, Aretha Franklin. What do you think about that?"

"I don't think those people ever left the church," I say. "We carry church in our hearts. It goes where we go. I couldn't any more leave church than leave my legs behind when I go out walking. Church is part of me."

"That's how I feel," says J. "That's what Mom used to say."

"That's how Shaleena lived. She loved the Lord in all things, in all ways and at all times. He lived His life through her."

"I'm happy when you talk that way, Aunt T."

"I'm happy to have you in my life, J."

"You sure about that?" the boy asks with a grin.

"It's part of God's plan," I say. "If it wasn't, it wouldn't be happening."

Big D

DOZENS of screaming young girls are waiting in the terminal when J and I arrive at the smaller of Dallas's two airports, Love Field. J, Damitra, and I have flown in on the private jet owned by Bishop Henry Gold, or perhaps owned by his Fellowship of Faith megachurch. Not that it makes any difference, since he and his church are one.

The girls are holding up signs:

"We love you, J Love!"

"J *is* Love!"

"J is my heart!"

"J Love's Dallas Fan Club."

There is no security so the girls practically knock us down. They are holding copies of his CDs—he has put out three—and pictures of him from magazines. They keep screaming his name and insisting on his autograph. They take his picture with their cell phones and give him bouquets of flowers. I see two girls give him notes with, I presume, their phone numbers. I do my best to maintain order, but I am overwhelmed.

Damitra, who has accompanied us on her father's plane, does far better than I at beating back the well-wishers. In an alarmingly loud voice, the singer, who is recognized by many of J's fans, screams, "Get back! You're crowding him! You're hurting him!"

But even the force of Damitra's no-nonsense command does not discourage the more determined. Those girls are still all over J.

These are the last days of August. We are here because Bishop Gold has arranged a concert at a megachurch in Houston. J Love is one of the featured artists. Bishop Gold will also be preaching. He sent his plane to Los Angeles to pick us up, and now we will spend a day in Dallas before Bishop, his wife, Damitra, and I fly down to Houston.

I am part of the entourage at J's request. J said he preferred that I come along with him, as his mother had so often done. At this point, I would have it no other way. I needed no further proof that J absolutely required supervision. Besides, my nephew Patrick and Naomi were happy to assume my church responsibilities.

The jet that carried us to Dallas had a bedroom in the back. When we had been in the air for a half hour or so, Damitra said she was tired and wanted to nap. That left J and me alone in the main cabin.

"Glad you're coming along, Aunt T," he said.

"I am too, baby. You know, Dallas is my hometown."

"Mama told me. And Andre's there?"

"We'll see him tonight."

J's mood had stayed good ever since his HIV test came back negative. On the other hand, I could hardly insist that Damitra be tested. That was not my business. My business, as far as I could decipher it, was to be a loving—and constant—presence in J's life. That of course would undoubtedly turn my own life upside down, but I had no choice. For all practical purposes, I was J's mom. I had to consider his welfare and his schooling. I had already made sure he had applied and was accepted to Crossroads, a highly rated private high school in Santa Monica, where he would commence his junior year next month.

As we flew over New Mexico, J put on his iPod earphones and listened to music. I closed my eyes and drifted. I dreamt about my childhood home in Dallas, my parents, and the struggles we endured. In my dream, my mother came to me and said, "My darling daughter, you are loved by me. You are loved by God. You are loved by those you serve." I opened my eyes feeling renewed and refreshed. But when I looked around, J was nowhere to be found. I figured he had probably just gone to the bathroom. I waited five, six, seven minutes. Then I became concerned.

I knocked on the bedroom door. The sound of my knock triggered scuffling noises. When the door opened I saw Damitra pretending to be asleep in bed and J by her side, reading the Bible. It all looked too good to be true.

I looked at J and J looked at me. He offered a small smile.

"Baby," I said, "why don't you keep me company out here?"

"Sure thing, Aunt T. There's a passage I'd like you to explain to me."

Back in the main cabin, we sat next to each other on a couch. His Bible was open to a passage in Leviticus.

"It's hard to understand, Aunt T," he said.

"Well, you tell me what you think it means, son."

He couldn't. I presumed that was because he hadn't read it. He had merely opened the Bible and found himself in Leviticus.

The passage was about leprosy.

"It's about disease," I told him. "A disease from the Old Testament days that some compare to AIDS today. People who had it were ostracized. They were cut off from society. Then Christ came and embraced those with the disease. Christ came and said all God's children are His beloved, no matter what their condition. God has no prejudice, God sees no separation between Himself and His creations."

"That's beautiful, Aunt T, maybe it's something I can rap about."

"Maybe so," I said.

But now the plane has landed and security from Fellowship of Faith has finally arrived. Two big guys are able to rescue J from his fans, one of whom has actually ripped his T-shirt. We're shepherded into a van with "Christ Lives at Fellowship of Faith" painted across the doors. It has to be 100 degrees, but the air-conditioning is blasting and we're finally on our way. As we drive through the neighborhood next to Love Field, my heartbeat quickens because this is the landscape of my childhood. In fact, we pass by the small house where I was raised. Through a wonderful quirk of fate, I know the present owners, a young couple named Marianne and Norman David who worship at the Church of the Nazarene, the same sanctuary where I was baptized a lifetime ago. I make a mental note to call the Davids before I leave for Houston.

The van drops J and me at a downtown hotel. Damitra, who will be staying with her parents, whispers something in J's ear.

"Okay," he says.

Okay what? I wonder.

We're given a two-bedroom suite.

In the early evening, J says, "Would you mind if I had dinner with Damitra and her parents?"

Would I mind?

"Not at all," I say, feeling that it is mighty peculiar that they have not invited me.

"The only thing," I say, "is that I'm having dinner with Andre, who'd very much like to see you."

"How about tomorrow? We don't leave till tomorrow night."

"Fine. But would you mind giving me the phone number at Damitra's parents in case I need to get hold of you?"

"No problem."

"Okay, baby, you have a wonderful time tonight. Let's meet back here at eleven."

"Why so early?"

"It's a weeknight," I say.

"Aunt T, do I really need a curfew?"

"Yes. Be here by eleven."

Andre picks me up at seven. We drive to a restaurant overlooking Turtle Creek, a woodsy section of the city just beyond downtown. Andre, at thirty-eight, has recently lived through a romantic trauma. He married a woman who was unfaithful to him. The divorce has been painful. He has also recently faced some professional challenges. He was hired by Bishop Gold to head a writing program set up by the church, only to have the program canceled. My nephew Patrick also worked for Bishop for a short time before becoming disillusioned with Fellowship of Faith.

"At least my job lasted longer than my marriage," Andre says as we order a few appetizers.

"Did Bishop ever tell you why the program was discontinued?" I ask.

"You don't get to talk to Bishop when you work for Fellowship of Faith. There are at least three levels of bureaucrats between him and your supervisors. The supervisors simply said funds were being diverted to other interests. It's a corporate culture. There are massive hirings often followed by massive firings. Whole divisions are created one day and whole divisions are destroyed the next. It's crazy."

"But you like your new teaching job."

"Love it. Great school. Great headmaster. Great schedule. Affords me lots of time to devote to my own writing. And the kids are very smart."

"They're lucky to have you teaching them, sweetheart," I say.

"I was hoping J would be coming along tonight. I wanted him to come speak to my class."

"He's busy."

"A girl?" Andre asks.

"How'd you know?"

"J's a chick magnet, Mom. He's at the age when his hormones are kicking in. And he's also a teen idol."

"He loves the Lord."

"Right now he may love the ladies more."

I nod my head in recognition of the truth. "I'm a little worried about him."

"Well, he's certainly crazy about you, Mom. You're the one who's gotten him through."

"I haven't gotten him through anything," I say. "I'm just along for the ride. And what I've seen so far is that there's more to the ride than meets the eye."

"What does that mean?"

"He's sexually active."

"I'd be surprised if he weren't. That just goes with the territory."

"I worry about his attitude towards women," I say. "They're there for the taking."

"It's their choice, isn't it?" asks my son.

"He can refuse."

"That's asking a lot of a teenage boy," says Andre.

I start to answer, but I don't. I decide it's better to let my son's words sink in.

I arrive back at the hotel at ten o'clock and watch the evening news. Bishop Gold is being interviewed about a new sports arena his church is building. It's big enough to house a professional ball team. He says that the church will lease it out not only for athletic events but concerts as well. "Christian concerts only," he says, speaking in his most authoritative voice. "What this community needs," he exclaims, "what this world needs is more Christian fellowship inspired by more Christian music."

I call Bishop's house to see how the evening went. Bishop's wife, Eugenia, answers the phone.

"Oh yes, Pastor Merci," she says, "we had a wonderful time. We adore your godson. Damitra borrowed our car to drive him back to the hotel. They should be there any minute."

"Thank you," I say.

"I look forward to seeing you tomorrow," adds Mrs. Gold.

"I didn't know you were coming to Houston. That's wonderful. We'll have a chance to chat."

"Indeed," she says in an accent that sounds slightly British.

Back to the news. Then the weather. Then the sports.

Now it's ten-thirty, now it's ten-forty-five. At eleven, still no J.

I call his cell phone only to have voice mail pick up.

I turn to the Word channel where, as fate would have it, last Sunday's service conducted by Bishop Gold is being rebroadcast. I turn off the TV.

Eleven-thirty. Eleven-forty-five. Call his cell again. Voice mail again.

Just when I feel my agitation quicken, the door opens and J appears with a smile on his face.

"Sorry, Aunt T, we stopped up for a cheeseburger."

"I thought Bishop and his wife served you dinner."

"They did, but they had fish and I hate fish. I hardly ate any of it."

"Oh," I say.

"You look like you don't believe me, Aunt T."

"Baby," I say, "I just want you to believe *me* when I say curfews are important."

"I believe you. But I wasn't driving. Damitra was. And she wanted to go to this burger place way out in Plano. She said they have the best burgers."

"I tried your cell," I say.

"Sorry, I turned it off."

"J," I say, switching subjects, "I need to say something to you, and I need to be direct."

"Okay."

"I think casual sex is a dangerous and immoral practice."

"I know that, Aunt T."

"I think sex is a sacred act. A beautiful act of love between two married people who are deeply in love."

"I understand that too. But I carry protection, just in case."

"Just in case *what*, J?"

"Things get out of hand."

"But, sweetheart, that's something you can control."

"Depends upon the girl."

"That's why some girls need to be avoided," I say.

"I'm trying my best to stick with the righteous ones, Aunt T. But it's the righteous ones who will surprise you."

EUGENIA SOMERSET GOLD

The flight from Dallas to Houston, normally only forty-five minutes or so, is delayed because of thunderstorms. We sit on the runway and wait. In the main cabin are myself, J, Damitra, Bishop Gold, and his wife, Eugenia.

J and Damitra are seated together on the couch talking. Bishop sits alone, talking intensely on his cell phone. He's worried that we won't land in time and the service will have to be canceled. "That'll cost us tens of thousands of dollars," he tells someone on the other end of the line.

Mrs. Gold and I are seated together in comfortable reclining seats. She seems eager to talk and I am quite willing to listen. I've never met the woman before and am curious about the first lady of the Fellowship of Faith, the country's largest African American church.

"Please call me Eugenia, Pastor," she says.

"Gladly. But only if you call me Albertina."

Eugenia is a thin woman of unusual intensity. She is fidgety. Her small hands are in constant motion. She is somewhere in her late fifties or early sixties and immaculately dressed in a tailored houndstooth St. John knit suit that I've seen at Neiman Marcus selling for $1,500. She wears two rings, an emerald-cut blue diamond and an oval sapphire, in addition to a discreet strand of cultured pearls that adorn her thin neck. Her skin is taut, her mouth narrow, and her eyes light brown, the same shade as her skin. Her accent is definitely English. When I ask her about it, she is grateful for the inquiry and a chance to explain her origins.

"I grew up in London," she tells me as the plane taxis. "My mother was an interior decorator who actually did work for the Queen Mother. She came from a distinguished family, the Somersets. That's my middle name. Her maiden name was Somerset. My father was a Jamaican preacher, the most famous on the island, who came to England with a reputation as a Christian scholar and charismatic figure in the evangelical movement. His church, while not as large as my husband's—few churches are—was nonetheless the most important church for people of color in Great Britain."

"So you were raised in London?"

"Yes, but of course, given my parents' work, we traveled the world."

"Where did you meet Bishop?"

"Oh, Albertina, that's a long story."

"With this rain delay," I say, looking out the window as we finally take off, "a long story may be just what the doctor ordered."

"You're kind to indulge me, Albertina."

"I'm genuinely curious."

"I can see that you're a genuine person. Well, the story begins, of all places, in Rome, where my father was conducting a seminar of young leaders in the evangelical movement. Have you been to Rome, Albertina?"

"Yes."

"Don't you adore it?"

"I do," I say.

"Mother was there as well. She was putting the finishing touches on an interior décor plan she had created for Contessa Barbieri, the founder of the famous handbag firm. At that point I was Mother's assistant."

"So you're a decorator as well?" I ask.

"Yes indeed. You've been to the Fellowship of Faith, I take it."

"I have."

"That's my handiwork."

"Most impressive," I say. In truth, I find the church's décor overdone with gold and gilded furnishings. But I keep my opinion to myself.

"Thank you. Anyway, I was with my parents in Rome when at the farewell dinner for the seminarians I happened to be seated next to Henry. He was a young man who had been brought up in one of the Carolinas, North or South, I never remember which. He was what the American Blacks like to call 'country,' but one immediately saw that he was a man of first-rate intelligence. He was articulate and, according to my father, he had great rhetorical gifts. But he was, to be kind, still unformed. Do you follow me, Albertina?"

"I'm with you, Eugenia."

"On the plus side, though, Henry proved to be a brilliant student. My father took him under his wing and he actually came to live in London for a month. That's when our relationship began. When my father saw that I was interested in Henry romantically, he said, 'This man has potential to be an important figure in the evangelical movement. But to do so, he must have vision. I'm not sure that he can develop the vision on his own. You must cultivate that vision in him, Eugenia. You must excite his ambition and help realize his potential.' And so I have. As you know, Albertina, I am the CEO of the church corporation."

"I didn't know."

"I've been blessed to have inherited my mother's great gift for business. When she passed ten years ago, she headed an interior decoration firm with offices in five European countries and a staff of sixty employees. The land for the Fellowship of Faith complex, some fifty acres, was bought with the money from the sale of Mother's company."

At this moment Bishop approaches his wife. He's distressed.

"The Houston airport is closed. They've got a storm there too. We're going to have to cancel."

"Canceling is not an option, Henry," says Eugenia, cool as a cucumber. "There's too much revenue involved. Simply tell the pilot to fly to Galveston and have a limo and police escort waiting."

"I'm not sure that can be arranged."

"I am. We can call the mayor."

"I don't know him," says Bishop.

"I do," Eugenia declares.

With that, Eugenia invites me to join her in the cockpit. "I want you to see, Albertina, how things get done around here."

Once inside, she instructs the pilot's assistant to get the mayor of Galveston on the phone. He does so in five or six minutes.

"Robert," she says, "Eugenia Somerset Gold. I take it that you and Julianne are in good health and enjoying your new library and den addition. It turned out divinely, didn't it, dear?"

The mayor says something before Eugenia replies, "It was

my pleasure. Decorating is my passion. But I'm calling you in an official capacity, Robert. You see we're thirty thousand feet in the air and have a minor problem."

She goes on to describe the problem. A half hour later, we land at a small airport in Galveston and a stretch limo, accompanied by two motorcycle policemen, gets us to the church on time.

The church used to be a basketball arena, and it's packed to the rafters. They say twenty thousand people are in attendance. Damitra and J are the opening acts for Bishop's rousing sermon. Fortunately, they were able to rehearse back in Dallas, so they're ready to go.

From my seat on the first row, I see that Damitra is a spirited singer. Her voice is excellent, reminiscent of Whitney Houston when Whitney was still a teenager. She has a clarity and confidence in the upper register unusual in someone so young. She also knows how to move her audience. She sings a song called "God Is Reaching Out to You." As far as I can tell, though, Damitra is reaching out to the young men in the audience. She dresses in a snug, revealing top of clingy material that glitters in the spotlight. Her skirt falls to an appropriate length but is even snugger than her top. God knows how she can even walk. But walk she does. She even manages to dance in that dress, and has no problem exciting the men, who seem happy to watch her blur the line between the sacred and the secular. They call for an encore. She sings, "You're Inside Me." The words say, "You're inside me, Jesus," but her tone says something else.

Next up is my godson. I can't help but be proud when he steps into the spotlight. This is his first performance since his mom died, and I'm glad for his willingness to get back out there.

I'm grateful to be witnessing his resurgence—because that's what it is. He's wearing a Popsicle-orange pin-striped seersucker sports coat at least two sizes too big for his thin frame and extra-baggy Evisu blue jeans with hand-painted accents and the cuffs turned up at least three inches. The back patches have "God Is Love" written in sequins. He's also got on a matching New Era white baseball cap with the Houston Astros logo written out in crystals and matching Christian Dior sunglasses. His shoes are customized cucumber-green Nike Air Force Ones. He steps to the mic. Behind him is a deejay who works with two turntables. The beat kicks in and J starts to rap:

> *I'm J Love*
> *In love*
> *With the God of love*
> *God above*
> *God who blesses us*
> *When we messing up*
> *When we guessing up*
> *If we heading for*
> *Wrong and right*
> *We turn to Him*
> *We yearn for Him*
> *Cause He don't do no judging*
> *He's all about loving*
> *Loving the winners*
> *Loving the sinners*
> *Loving the saints*
> *And those who ain't*
> *So get your praise on*
> *And praise Him for days*
> *Praise in all ways*

When you shopping for hoodies
Or eating sweet goodies
Keep God on your mind
And let yourself find
The right motivation
For righteous salvation
So kick it with God
And be down with His mob
No gangstas, no crime
Just straight-love all the time
Say, kick it with God
And be down with His mob
No gangstas, no crime
Just love all the time

As J keeps up the refrain—"No gangstas, no crime/Just love all the time"—everyone is waving their arms in the air, especially the young people. J is turning it out.

He's back for an encore. They just won't let him go. His next rap, "Jumpin' for Jesus," has everyone bouncing up and down until it feels like the windows are about to shatter and the floor is about to collapse. He finally leaves the stage but the thunderous applause doesn't stop until he returns for a second encore, "God Is the Good Groove." That groove is J's best, a happy hip-hop beat that keeps everyone up and dancing. It's a masterful performance.

When Bishop Gold steps forth the crowd is already worked up, and his words, spoken eloquently and with a finely honed sense of propulsive rhythm, hit their mark. I've heard him give many variations of this sermon, but tonight he's especially on his game. His message is that God wants you not only to be spiritually rich, but materially rich as well. God's love is abundant and so are His worldly blessings. Ask and you will receive. Of course Bishop underlines his theme with many dramatic illustrations. They all lead, however, to one conclusion: worship God and you'll be rewarded with wealth.

Personally, I don't believe it, not for a minute. The truth—at least the truth from my viewpoint—is that Jesus cautioned us about worldly wealth. Just read Matthew 19:24, where Jesus says that it's easier for a camel to pass through the eye of a needle than for a rich man to enter the kingdom of God.

The more Bishop preaches, "We can all get rich now," the more I hear Jesus preaching, "Blessed are the poor in spirit; for theirs is the kingdom of heaven." Why are we following a gospel of prosperity when the man at the heart of the Gospel, Jesus Christ, the man who *is* the Gospel, lived His life on earth as exemplary pauper, preaching to the disenfranchised? I don't know of a miracle in which Jesus makes a poor man rich or turns dust to diamonds. But this is me, and these are my private thoughts. This is Bishop's night, and these are his public thoughts. He is certainly getting over. The twenty thousand in attendance like what they hear. The preaching plan, of course, is clear: Bishop is building up to the pitch. Give to God and God will give to you.

"Let's start with the humblest among us," he says, "because they are blessed as well. Let's start with those able to give ten dollars." From there he moves to fifty, then to a hundred, then to the most blessed of all, the contributors who can give a thousand or more.

The line of such contributors amazes me. He has worked up the crowd to the point where it seems as though everyone is emptying their pockets, everyone eager to buy God's grace.

For my part, I do not contribute, not out of stinginess but simply because I don't know where the money's going. I don't believe in uninformed giving. I also wonder about the financial arrangement between Bishop and J. I know Bishop has paid all our expenses and treated us royally, but what is J's percentage of the money raised tonight? It's a question I want to raise.

When the service is over, the young girls move toward the front, where J was sitting next to Damitra during her dad's sermon. I see many of them handing him cards, presumably with their phone numbers. He's cordial and friendly to all of them. After fifteen minutes or so, Damitra whisks him away to a private room. I follow them and congratulate them on their excellent performances.

After an hour of autograph signing and picture taking, we leave the arena in a stretch limo—myself, J, Damitra, Bishop, and Eugenia.

"Wonderful service," says Bishop. "Time to celebrate."

The celebration takes place in a fancy restaurant in downtown Houston. Steak and lobster for everyone. Before the elaborate meal, Bishop offers a short and, it seems to me, perfunctory prayer. He devours his food.

"J and I have been invited to a party that the youth choir is giving in our honor," says Damitra. "Do you mind if we go, Daddy?"

"Not at all, sweetheart."

"Be back at the hotel by eleven-thirty," I say.

"Aunt T," says J, "it's almost ten now. That's impossible."

"No later than midnight then," I insist.

He rolls his eyes and nods his head.

"I'm serious, J," I say. *"Midnight."*

After they leave, Eugenia says to me, "You're right to establish boundaries, Albertina. Boundaries are important."

"I think so," I say.

"I try to tell Henry that," Eugenia continues, "but that daughter of ours has him wrapped around her little finger."

Bishop changes the subject. He wants to know if Eugenia checked the receipts.

"Of course, darling," she says. "Excellent night."

I'm aware that, given my presence, she prefers not to give a total. I don't say a word because, in truth, it isn't my business. But J is. And even though it's uncomfortable for me, I find the courage to bring up the uncomfortable subject of his compensation.

"Bishop," I say, "as you know, I've become J's guardian. And as such, I will be overseeing his finances. His mother's lawyer told me that she had left him her modest savings. And I know there is a considerable sum in his own bank account from the sales of CDs and his concert appearances. But during services such as these, Bishop, I'm wondering how he's compensated."

"My dear pastor," Gold is quick to answer, "these are questions for my wife. She is our chief financial officer. You see, we all work for Eugenia."

I turn to Eugenia, who is gently stirring her cup of Earl Grey tea.

"Your godson is a blessing to our ministry," she says, "and as such we pay him an honorarium."

"Does it vary according to the nightly contributions?" I ask.

"It's consistent and generous. Neither he nor his mother ever found reason to question our generosity." Now Eugenia's voice is stern and cold.

"Your generosity, Eugenia, is not the question. I'm sure you and your husband, as Christians, are generous to a fault. This is a matter of professional compensation."

Eugenia focuses her eyes on mine. She looks at me forcefully and speaks deliberately.

"I wish to be clear, Albertina. I know something about you, and I have great respect for your independence. When my husband went to great lengths to establish a Los Angeles mega-church, which you were able to block, I watched those negotiations from afar, and I was impressed with your strategic thinking. I do not underestimate you, not for a second. But in the matter of your godson, I feel you are out of your league. He is a talent who is playing on the national stage. He requires the kind of direction that our professional gospel management division has to offer. For his own good, I suggest you not only allow us to see after his career, but even more importantly, I encourage you to back us when we urge him to move to Dallas. That way he'll be closer to the people he needs the most. I hope you agree."

I take a couple of deep breaths, close my eyes to say a silent prayer, and then address both Bishop and his take-charge wife.

"I'm afraid that I don't agree," I say. "I don't agree at all."

"WE'RE ON ThE AiR WiTh PaSToR ALBERTiNa MERCi!"

This is *Just Jazz,* and I'm your host Clifford Bloom. We're coming to you tonight on public radio from the University of Dallas. And we're on the air with Pastor Albertina Merci! Good evening, it's an honor to have you on our program."

"It's my honor, Clifford. I'm delighted to be with you."

"Most of you, of course, know Albertina Merci from her famous rhythm and blues recordings. Her hit from the sixties, 'Sanctified Blues,' is a classic of the genre. But what you may not know is that Albertina has a strong background in jazz. Tonight we'll get to explore the jazz side of this great artist. But before we do, let's give a listen to a song that reconciles, as no song has done before or since, the secular and sacred. Here's Albertina Merci's marvelous 'Sanctified Blues.' "

As the song plays, Clifford turns to me, takes my hand, and says, "Thanks for accepting the invitation."

"I'm loving it, Clifford. I'm having a ball."

Clifford is one of my best friends. I met him back in Los Angeles, where he was a famous jazz deejay and scholar. He's also a Jew who, in his late sixties, converted to Christianity and joined House of Trust. There was a time when he was interested in marrying me. That was about the same time when Mr. Mario came into my life and proposed as well. I was torn but decided marriage to either man wasn't right. Then Clifford accepted a job as head of jazz studies at the University of Dallas. He wanted me to move here, but I couldn't leave my congregation. When he heard I was back from Houston for a day, he arranged to have me on his show.

"That was the immortal 'Sanctified Blues,'" he now says, "written and sung by our guest, Albertina Merci. Or Pastor Merci, I should say."

"I prefer plain old Albertina," I say.

"Albertina, I know your roots are in jazz. Tell us about that."

"Certainly, Clifford. I've lived in Detroit, and Detroit, as you know, is a serious jazz city. When I was a teenager Mr. Berry Gordy himself took me under his wing and introduced me to Miss Billie Holiday, who was singing at the Flame Bar and Showroom. I was singing a little like Billie, but she told me to develop my own style. I remember seeing Betty Carter at Baker's Keyboard Lounge and being impressed by her own unique style. You see, Clifford, that's what jazz taught me, that we each have a unique voice and a unique way to express it. I loved singing jazz."

"But then you made a transition to rhythm and blues."

"Well, I know you're a scholar of this music, Clifford, and Lord knows you have a greater knowledge of it than I do, but my feeling is that there are more similarities than differences between rhythm and blues and jazz."

"In recent years, after your ordination as a minister, Albertina, you've made gospel records. Is gospel mixed up with R&B and jazz?"

"I'd put it another way, Clifford. I'd say that God is mixed up in everything. The music I was raised on, the music I once heard you call the holy trinity—blues, jazz, and gospel—all comes from the Lord. All great gifts come from Him. It was our people's way of expressing our soul—our joys and sorrows, our hopes and dreams. Mahalia Jackson, the greatest gospel singer of all time, sang with Duke Ellington. Mavis Staples, another fabulous gospel artist, has lots of rhythm and blues hits. When I sing, for example, I sing for the glory of God. I sing to raise people's spirits and inspire faith. When I'm listening to Ella Fitzgerald sing "Body and Soul," my faith is inspired. It's not gospel, but it invokes the beauty of God, just like the sun setting over the ocean, or at dawn when the black sky turns to misty blue."

"Well, folks, you can see that Albertina Merci is not only one of my favorite singers, but my favorite preacher. Let's go back and listen to another one of her great hits. Here's 'Stay Out of the Kitchen,' recorded on the great Stax label out of Memphis, Tennessee."

After the show, Clifford takes me to dinner at a quiet Chinese restaurant in Richardson, close to his home.

"That was the best show of the year," he tells me after we order egg drop soup and barbecue spare ribs. "You're a scintillating guest."

"I'm a chatterbox," I say.

"You're a jewel."

"Thank you, but I want to hear about your job at the university, Clifford. Tell me about your new life in Dallas."

"The jazz studies program is in full swing. Life here is good, but it's lonely without you, Albertina."

I don't want to encourage Clifford's romantic leanings, but neither do I want to discourage his friendship. He's a beautiful man with a loving heart. And because he's a true friend, I decide to confide in him.

"My life isn't lonely, Clifford, but it sure is complicated."

"How so?"

"I've become the mother of a fifteen-year-old teenage boy who just happens to be a superstar in the world of gospel."

"This is J Love?"

"The one and only," I say.

"I know he's talented, and I know he's something of a heart-throb. Part of your job must be keeping the girls away."

"I'm not sure what my job is," I confess.

"And I presume he has no father," says Clifford.

"Long gone."

"No man to establish the rule of moral law."

"Bishop Gold and his wife, not to mention their daughter, are looking to manage him."

"And you're against it?" he asks.

"I'm skeptical of their motives."

"Does he want to move to Dallas?"

"I don't think the boy knows what he wants, Clifford. He just lost the mother he loves, and now he's back into a world where every teenage girl seems to love him. How does he resist those girls? What gives him the strength? I want to help him. I want to guide him, but I don't want to impose unrealistic restrictions that will only provoke him further."

"Well, if he wants to move here, Albertina, maybe you should move here as well. That way you could keep an eye on him. And I wouldn't at all mind getting involved with the young man in a supervisory role. I've always had good rapport with teenagers. I think I understand them, and I think I could be an instrument in helping you raise him."

I realize Clifford's offer is well intentioned, but I also see his personal agenda. Of course I'm flattered—what woman wouldn't be?—but Clifford is not the solution to J's problems.

"I can't leave Los Angeles," I say. "And I don't think I can leave J here in Dallas. My home is in California, and his home is with me."

"As long as you think it'll work."

"It'll work as long as I do God's will."

"And how do you know when that's the case?" Clifford asks.

"I pray. And right now I'm praying 24/7."

CROSSROADS

TELL ME MORE about Crossroads, Aunt T?" says J.

"It's a private school in Santa Monica. I know the headmaster and several of the teachers. I think you'll like it, J," I say. "They have a national reputation."

"Is it a Christian school?" he asks.

"There are Christians who attend. Also Jews, Muslims, and a wide variety of students. I want you to get a good across-the-board education. Crossroads has a national reputation for excellence."

I've thought about a Christian school, but I fear the Christian schools are too strict and narrow in their approach. I see Christian schools as something against which J might rebel. I want J to love his education and look forward to each class. I want his curiosity excited and his imagination broadened.

Tuition at Crossroads is sky high, but it's worth it.

Steering J away from Dallas hasn't been difficult. Bishop

Gold has come on too soon and too strong, insisting that J make the move immediately. J didn't want to move so quickly. Eugenia insisted as well. She even gave J a projection of his six-figure income over the next twelve months. "With the Fellowship of Faith talent management team behind you," she said, "you're guaranteed a one-hundred-fifty-thousand-dollar income."

"That's good money," I said to J when he told me about his meeting with Eugenia.

"Do you think I should take it?" he asked.

"Sweetheart," I said, "I think you should think about who you want guiding your career."

"My mother guided my career, Aunt T, and now that she's gone, I want you to guide it."

"I'm not sure of how good a guide I'll be," I confessed.

"You're honest," he said. "And I know you love me."

"You're right on both scores, baby. But when it comes to bookings and performance fees, you need professional advice. You could use a good lawyer."

"Remember the lawyer you introduced me to in Dallas, the one who was married to your niece who died so young?"

"Bob Blakey."

"Is he big-time?"

"I should say so. He represents Maggie Clay."

"Wow. And you trust him?"

"With my life."

"Well," said J, "maybe he could help me. Besides, I don't even know how much I'll be working. I'll definitely fly out to do some concerts on weekends, but with this new school and everything, I'd like to settle in before I do too much traveling."

"I like your thinking, son," I said.

"You'll call that Blakey guy then?"

"I'll do better than that, J. I'll have Bob come to L.A. to meet with you."

"Meet with *us*, Aunt T. I want you in on everything."

J likes Bob from the get-go.

We're having lunch at Stay Out of the Kitchen, where Mr. Mario has prepared a special carrot salad for the meeting. J's happy to see that Bob has answers to all the questions that Mario and I are asking.

"The gospel youth market is bigger than you would imagine," says Bob. "There are dozens of megachurches—black, white, and Hispanic—that provide huge venues for concerts. As you know, getting J a booking isn't a problem. He's an established star. But negotiating fees is another matter."

"Couldn't you do that?" J asks.

"I could."

"Well, that'd be great. Aunt T can do the bookings and then you can cut the deals."

I'm about to say, "Wait a minute. Aunt T is a little busy these days being the minister of her church. Aunt T has hospital visits to make, baptisms to organize, Bible classes to conduct. Aunt T never stops running from one church function to another." But I don't say it because I think that, for all my other responsibilities, this is one I must accept. Besides, Patrick and Naomi have done a beautiful job of taking over my duties. The congregation has met J and they understand my situation. Everyone at House of Trust is encouraging me to do whatever I can to help this boy.

So if J is willing, even eager, to give me control over his bookings that will mean I will oversee his schedule. If his schoolwork is going well, I can book him accordingly; if it isn't,

I can pull back on his weekend concerts. Besides, working with Bob Blakey affords me a sense of complete confidence. *Shaleena can rest easy,* I think to myself, *her son will be in good hands.*

Crossroads does not have an impressive campus. It sits in an industrial section of Santa Monica just off Interstate 10. The buildings look thrown together; some are modern, some shabby. They face a concrete alley. There are few trees or shrubs. The ambience is gray, not green. But once you go inside, you feel the enthusiasm of the students and the faculty. The kids can call their teachers by their first names, and the teachers are accessible. Nonconformity is tolerated. Individual thinking is encouraged. The classroom discussions are lively and open-ended. Dogma is discouraged. So is intolerance. The kids are given projects that bring them out into the community for worthwhile causes.

"It's a long way from Memphis," said J when I first took him over to Crossroads, "but it seems pretty cool."

"These are kids who probably don't know too much about gospel rap stars," I told him. "Does that bother you?"

"No, it's better that way. I'll be just like everyone else. I get tired of everyone making a fuss over me."

It's not a normal school," J says after his first week.

It's Friday afternoon and we've gone to Stay Out of the Kitchen for an early dinner. After fixing us an extravagant vegetable plate set off with soy-meat tacos, Mario joins us. J is famished and wolfs down the food in no time.

"What's not normal about it?" asks Mario.

"Lots of the kids act like hippies. Then a lot of them have famous actors and actresses for mothers and fathers. One kid's dad owns a movie studio. One owns a chain of newspapers."

"Are the kids accepting of you, J?" I ask.

"Some are, some aren't. It's kinda cliquish."

"Aren't all schools?" asks Mario.

J says, "Sure. I guess I feel this way 'cause I'm new."

"You don't feel welcome?"

"The teachers are cool. Real cool. I'm taking a course on jazz."

"That's great," says Mario. "You'll be learning about your own culture."

"Most of the time we're listening to records," says J. "I like that."

"What is it about the school that you don't like?"

"Word got out that I was a rapper, and so everyone started coming around asking about my flow. They wanted me to start free-styling in the schoolyard."

"Well, did you?" I ask.

"Not really. They think I'm like T.I. or maybe Talib Kweli. They don't know anything about gospel rap."

"And you don't want to tell them?" I ask.

"I just wanna go to school and be normal," says J. "I wanna find my way before I start performing for them."

"I agree with you, baby," I say.

"I also need to kick up my reading skills," adds J. "They're giving me real fat books about history and art."

"I can help you with that, son," says Mario. "I'm a pretty good reader. Matter of fact, I once worked as a tutor for kids taking their college boards. I got some techniques you could use. You interested?"

"No doubt," says J.

"Sounds like you're doing fine, sweetheart," I say.

"I got invited to a couple of parties, Aunt T. Some of the Crossroads kids are getting together this weekend. Since I'm not working, I figure I could go."

"Long as we get started on this reading program," says Mario.

"And as long as the parties have adult supervision," I add.

"I'm sure they do," says J.

"I'm not," I say. "I want to talk to the parents of the party givers."

"I don't have their numbers."

"Well, find them, son, and I'll make the calls."

I make the calls. One is Bret Sapperstein. It's probably easier to reach the president of the United States than Bret Sapperstein. Sapperstein is a Hollywood bigwig. I'm not sure what he does, but it takes at least a half-dozen phone calls to get him on the line. It's only when I say it's about his son Nigel that he picks up.

"Mr. Sapperstein," I say, "this is Albertina Merci. My godson J has been invited to a party at your home this weekend and I just want to make sure there'll be adult supervision."

"A party?" he asks. "I guess Nigel's giving a party. I'll be in New York, but yes, the housekeeper will be on duty."

That evening I inform J that the Sapperstein party is off limits. When I explain why, he says, "Aunt T, I'm new at this school, and I don't want the kids to think I'm a nerd. What will I tell them when they ask why I didn't show at the party?"

"Tell them that your aunt wouldn't let you, sweetheart. Tell them that your aunt is a nerd."

"You're no nerd, Aunt T."

"Neither are you, baby, and even if you were, I'd love you the same. Try not to worry about what others think."

"What about the other party?"

"I'm waiting to hear back from the girl's mother."

The girl, Joyce Gooding, is African American. Her father is a well-known criminal lawyer and her mother, Edna, was once a city councilwoman.

"Of course both my husband and I will be here," says Edna Gooding when she returns my call. "We live up in Baldwin Hills, and we're delighted that your godson will be coming to Joyce's party. You're welcome to join us."

Baldwin Hills, often called the black Beverly Hills, is an exclusive neighborhood only a few miles from my house.

"I'd love to, Mrs. Gooding," I say, "but I think my godson would die of humiliation."

My godson is thrilled that I allow him to attend the Gooding party. He isn't thrilled that the curfew is midnight.

"Midnight is way too early, Aunt T. Midnight is when the party is just getting started."

"Your party, son, will be ending at eleven-thirty. That's when you'll be walking out the door. Patrick will pick you up and drive you back."

"Don't I get a grace period?"

"No. You get a curfew, and the curfew's midnight."

Come the night of the party, Mario and I are playing Scrabble at my dining room table. I've asked him over to keep me company. I want to be up when J arrives home. Much to my delight, J comes through the front door right at midnight. He's smiling broadly.

"Have fun, sweetheart?" I ask him.

"No doubt, Aunt T," he says.

"Come tell us about the party," urges Mario.

J walks into the dining room. He's wearing a hoody done up in purple-and-black stripes. When I ask him who was at the party, he looks away as he answers.

"Just some kids from school," he says.

"How was the music?" asks Mario.

"They had a deejay," J replies.

"Any good?" asks Mario.

"Pretty good," says J.

J is uncomfortable standing there in front of us. "Enough of these questions," I tell Mario. "The boy's tired. Let him go to sleep."

J goes off to his bedroom.

"I'm worried," says Mario when J is gone.

"Why?" I ask. "He was home on time. He met his curfew."

"Arriving home on time is one thing, Albertina. But arriving home stoned is something else."

"How do you know?"

"Been there. Done that."

"You could be wrong."

"But I ain't. His eyes were red and that big grin of his said, 'I'm high.'"

"How can I know for sure, Mario?"

"You can start by asking him directly. Ask him first thing tomorrow morning."

D id you smoke marijuana?" I ask J first thing in the morning. I've prepared us a pre-church breakfast.

"What makes you think so, Aunt T?"

"Mario thought so."

"You believe him?"

"I'll believe you because I know your mama taught you to be honest."

"Well"—he hesitates, then falls into silence.

"Well, *what?*" I want to know.

"I had a puff or two."

"Were you high when you got home?"

"A little."

"Had you ever smoked it before?"

"No, but I've been offered."

"So why did you accept this time?"

"Saw no reason not to."

"Weren't Joyce's parents around?"

"They were inside. The party was out on the patio. We were just chillin' out there, looking at the view. You can see downtown L.A. from the patio. It's amazing up there."

"And someone offered you pot?"

"They were passing around a joint, that's all. It was no big thing."

"And everyone was getting high?"

"Look, Aunt T, I didn't keep track of who was smoking and who wasn't."

"But you were."

"I already said I was. I'm sorry."

"You're also grounded."

"For how long?"

"A month."

"But I have a concert in Atlanta next week."

"We're canceling it."

"You can't, Aunt T."

"I can and I will."

"This isn't fair," T says. "You didn't say you didn't want me smoking grass."

"I didn't have to. It's illegal."

"I thought it was legal in California."

"For medical purposes. With a doctor's prescription."

"Aunt T, you're getting too strict. I don't like it."

"I understand that, J. Every teenager wants complete freedom. But complete freedom at your age leads to complete chaos. If you smoke pot, you're going to pay the consequences."

"I don't like this situation," he says.

"Neither do I."

"You were the one who sent me to this school. Kids at this school use drugs."

"J," I say, "kids at every school use drugs."

J doesn't respond.

"I want to go to Atlanta and do my show," he says. "If I don't go it'll cost me a lot of money."

"I know, but you have to understand, son, that there are rules that cannot be broken."

"But what if I don't like the rules, Aunt T?"

"You'll have to learn to live with them anyway."

"What if I make all As on my tests at school? What if I bring home a perfect report card? Will you stop being so strict?"

"We're not negotiating, J. You're grounded until further notice."

You were tough," says Mario when I tell him what happened. "Tough on the outside, soft on the inside."

"Can you stay tough?" he asks me. "Or do you want me to intercede?"

"To do what?"

"Knock some sense into the kid."

"Physically?" I ask Mario.

"When it's appropriate."

"I'm against corporal punishment."

"Spare the rod—"

"That quote is misunderstood. There's enough violence in our community without doing violence to our children."

"Please, Albertina, that line of thought leads to indulgence."

"Do you think I'm indulging the boy?"

"I didn't say that."

"Then let me do what I think needs to be done."

"You've been doing that," says Mario, "and he keeps testing you. He thinks he can get you to change your mind."

"Well, he can't."

"You sure?"

"Yes, I'm sure," I say. "I'm not changing my mind."

CHANGING MY MIND

TEENAGERS make adults crazy.

When I was a teenager, I surely made my parents crazy. I dated a few guys they didn't consider suitable. My folks were right, but I dated them anyway. It wasn't that I was rebellious, but I was young and overly impressed by pretty eyes and slick styles. I know that my mom and dad, beautiful and God-loving people, died a thousand deaths as I ignored their warnings, but they understood that young people have to make their own mistakes. I made many. The ability to evaluate men and see into their souls did not come quickly to me. I've had challenging marriages. I've had heartaches. I've lived through long and rough patches of loneliness and dejection. At the same time, those were the periods when I grew closer to God. I learned that when the world doesn't seem to love you, He always does. When the world rejects you, He never does. His love is the real

love, the eternal love that transcends the temporary. He is forever.

He is the lover of my soul, and it is to Him that I turn when I
feel myself torn in two directions. It is His will and wisdom that
I seek. It is Him whom I call upon after reading a letter that arrives at the House of Trust a week after J came home high. The
letter reads:

Dear Albertina,

Some time back I read about you and your church in
Jet magazine, and I'm trusting that I've found the right
mailing address. It's been way too long since we've spoken,
but as you can see from the letterhead I've been blessed
with a new position, Executive Director of the AAAMC, the
Atlanta African American Music Celebration. I have fond
memories of when I worked as Ray Charles's road manager
and you were the lead Raelette. How time flies!

I'm writing for your help. Our festival features the
greatest artists in jazz, R&B, and gospel. I understand that
your godson, J Love, will be headlining one of our gospel
concerts but that you have some reservations about his
appearance. I'm hoping you'll reconsider, Albertina, since
his concert is sold out and will certainly be the most
popular of the entire weekend.

As you know, the Lord works in mysterious and
miraculous ways. I say that because earlier today we
learned that Gladys Knight, our R&B headliner, had to
cancel for personal reasons. I was thinking how wonderful
it would be if you could replace Gladys with an evening of
your great R&B hits at the Georgia Superdome. I know
you're a woman of God now, Albertina, but you've always

been a woman of God, even when you were singing the blues, especially your fabulous "Sanctified Blues." If you call today, I'm sure we can quickly come to terms. Everyone here is eager to have you—and, of course, J as well. Who knows, this could be the rejuvenation of your R&B career, Albertina. All the great ladies of soul—from Ruth Brown to Mavis Staples—revived their careers in their golden years. And I see no reason why that couldn't be the case for the great Albertina Merci!

Your friend,
Parker Mint

Parker Mint . . . Lord, have mercy!

He's a character all right. Parker had been road manager for Jackie Wilson and James Brown before he hooked up with Ray. He's a smart cookie who, late in life, went to college to get a degree in business management. Parker was highly efficient at his job. At last count he had been through five wives. I know the last two. In fact, I know more about Parker Mint than most people. One thing I do know, though, is that the man is honest. And I can't help but be impressed by how he's running this big-time Atlanta music festival.

Headlining the Georgia Superdome is nothing to sneeze at. Dr. Billy Graham and Bishop T. D. Jakes have preached in the Superdome before eighty thousand people. Aretha Franklin and the Rolling Stones have performed there. And to replace Gladys Knight, one of the greatest singers of all time, is beyond an honor. It is, I admit to myself, a dream.

"Do it," says Justine. "Do it and I'll be cheering you from the first row."

I call Justine because, as my best friend, she always speaks her mind. And besides, I have a notion she'll push me into calling Parker Mint. Justine wants to push me back into the spotlight. I call her because maybe I want that push.

"Here's the problem, Justine," I say. "Parker's only giving me that slot because they want J. He's using me."

"And you're using him. And we're all using each other. That's life, Albertina. You know it as well as I do."

"But I was firm with J in telling him that he couldn't go to Atlanta."

"Well, this is different," says Justine. "You'll be going with J. You'll be able to watch his every move."

"I'm uncomfortable that I'm booked as part of the rhythm and blues show. I'd be more comfortable singing in the gospel concert."

"Be realistic, girl. Your reputation is in R&B. You had lots of R&B hits. That's what you're known for. Your fans have been missing you. I've been telling you that for years. Well, here's proof."

"What am I going to wear?"

"I'll come to L.A. a week before and we'll go shopping."

"And the band? Where will the musicians come from and how will we get ready in time?"

"Excuses, excuses, excuses. I am certain that Mr. Parker Mint will see to all that. He's a professional, you're a professional, and he'll find you professional musicians. Stop running from this rainbow, Albertina. It's the chance of a lifetime."

"And my church?"

"Everyone in your congregation will run out and buy a plane ticket to Atlanta to see you perform. Your people love you. They'll be tickled pink to see you sing at the Georgia Superdome."

"I feel funny about it."

"Look, Albertina, Della Reese has her church and her show business career, both at the same time. There's no reason you can't."

"Now you have me going back into show business full-time."

"I'd love it. I'd travel with you, honey. I'd do your wardrobe."

"What about your job at Wal-Mart?"

"I'd quit it in a hot second."

"And how would your devoted husband feel about your running off on some concert tour?"

"He'd understand. He'd have to. It's show business."

"What's so great about show business?"

"I don't know, but everyone wants to be in it. Including me. And, if you're honest with yourself, including you, too."

I don't call Parker Mint, but instead take the rest of the day to think about what Justine has said. When J comes home from school, I don't say anything to him. He immediately goes to his room, where he busies himself with homework. He's determined to make As on every test so I'll change my mind about Atlanta. Mario's tutoring sessions have paid off. His reading has improved dramatically. During dinner, J tells me about a film course he's taking at Crossroads that examines African American images in the history of Hollywood. He's also taking an applied jazz course where he's playing drums and doing extremely well.

"I love the school you picked out for me, Aunt T," he says. "The thing that blows my mind is that even though the school's mainly white, they offer more courses on black subjects than schools that are mostly black."

"I was hoping you'd find it stimulating."

"Got an A on my first English paper. It was about Ernest

Hemingway. I like Hemingway 'cause he wrote short sentences and is easy to understand. He had a beat. When you read him, Aunt T, you feel the beat."

"That's great, J. I like that you're reading more."

"And I've started writing again."

"Wonderful, baby."

"In fact, Aunt T, I wrote a rap about my mom. And you."

"I'm flattered, sweetheart."

"I was mad at you about grounding me and all, but then I started praying and seeing things differently. All of a sudden, these words started flowing. I wrote 'em down real quick. Wanna hear them?"

"Of course."

J starts in, rapping in rhyme to a tight rhythm:

> *You lose a friend*
> *You lose a mother*
> *Maybe out there*
> *You lose a brother*
> *You all messed up*
> *You're 'fraid and alone*
> *Nowhere to go*
> *Ain't got no home*
> *You wander here*
> *You wander there*
> *You ain't sure*
> *If anyone cares*
> *Cry at night*
> *Scream and cuss*
> *You wanna escape*
> *You've had enough*
> *But then a voice*

Whispers in your ear
"God is here
No need to fear."
A friend, an aunt,
An angel comes your way
Saying, "I believe in you
It's gonna be okay."
So just hang on in
When things get rough
Cause the Spirit is real
And the Spirit is tough
'Cause no matter how bad
Negativity attacks
You can be sure
God's got your back
Say, no matter how bad
Negativity attacks
You can be sure
God's got your back.

When he's through, my eyes are wet with tears. The words touch my heart. J's sentiment touches my heart. Despite the discipline I've had to impose, despite the resentment he's been feeling, his sweetness and appreciation still find a voice. I'm both amazed and moved. I've underestimated his spiritual maturity. He's truly a special servant.

But then I have another thought: Is he trying to butter me up so I'll change my mind and let him go to Atlanta? I don't like entertaining this thought. It doesn't feel good to have it float through my mind. I dismiss it. J is a sincere boy. He's always been that way. His personality won me over when he was a toddler. He's always showered affection on his mother and his mother's friends. People have always felt moved to shower affection on him. It's no different now that he is older, only more complex because he's a young man and the affection is coming from young women. The affection has taken on a sexual slant, but that's life. That's the human condition. That's when young people mix up romance, affection, and physical intimacy. It's understandable, but it's also dangerous. And it's difficult to understand when you're a teenage boy with raging hormones.

Clearly J is going through a period of raging hormones. He's vulnerable to the aggressive advances of young girls. I have compassion for him; I have compassion for the young girls who swoon when he raps; I have compassion for the parents of the young girls who worry about their daughters' self-respect when they engage in casual sex. I can find compassion for everyone, but that still doesn't resolve the dilemma. How do I draw boundaries for this boy? How do I make sure he doesn't get a girl pregnant? How do I instill within him a sense of morality? How do I let him know that smoking marijuana—a seemingly harmless act—can cloud his thinking and compromise his behavior? When he's argued that a little wine or pot helps loosen your inhibitions, I've tried to explain that inhibitions are the very things you do not want to loosen. You want to keep your wits about you. You want to be able to discern what is right and what is wrong.

Yet here he is, telling me about his good grades and reading me a rap that honors my place in his life. How can I not hug him and thank him for that gift? How can I not take him into my confidence and tell him how I've been asked to replace Gladys Knight as a headliner at the same event where he too has been booked?

"That's so cool, Aunt T," he says. "Does that mean we can go there together? I'd love that. I've never seen you sing R&B."

"You did when you were a very little boy, J. I remember your dad's brother brought you to a Ray Charles concert when your mom and I were Raelettes. You came backstage and we took a picture of you staring up at Ray and Ray smiling that big grin at you."

"I still have that picture. I love it! Uncle Gates took me to that concert."

"That's right," I say. "Gates Turner. He was a promoter back then. He was promoting wrestling matches."

"And R&B concerts too. He knew Don King. I met Don King. One time Uncle Gates took me to a big prize fight."

"That's the same uncle you lost track of, isn't it?" I ask.

"Last time my mom and I heard from him he was in Detroit. I think he was just getting out of jail. Mom, being Mom, helped him out with some money."

"She was generous that way."

"Never could turn anyone down."

"Well," I say, "I'm finding it hard to turn down this invitation to Atlanta."

"Why would you, Aunt T?"

"Been a good spell since I've sung R&B."

"Mom said singing the blues is like riding a bike. You don't ever forget."

I smile. "Not everyone approves of ministers singing the blues."

"How 'bout Al Green. Isn't he a minister?"

"He's a right reverend."

"Well, there you go," says J. "If Al Green can do it, so can you. He doesn't love the Lord less because he's singing love songs, does he?"

"I can't speak to his relationship to the Lord, but I do believe you can love the Lord with all your heart no matter what your job."

"Come on, Aunt T. You wanna go to Atlanta, and so do I. I promise I won't take even one sip of wine. If I'm in a room where they're smoking pot, I'll walk out. I won't inhale. I won't even risk a contact high. I swear. Just think about it, Aunt T—Atlanta will be the perfect place for me to debut the rap I wrote for you. You'll be there to hear it!"

"I'd like that."

"You'll also like the Georgia Superdome."

"I *am* eager to see what it's like to sing before eighty thousand people."

"I did it last year, and it was a blast, Aunt T! You'll love it, and your fans will love you! What'd you tell them? What did you say?"

"What can I say?"

"Yes," says J.

"Then yes it is."

"Yes! Yes! Yes!" J is jumping for joy.

"GOD'S GOT YOUR BACK"

ALBERTINA MERCI, how lovely to see you here," says Eugenia Somerset Gold, as we bump into each other in the hotel lobby on the Friday before the big concert. "Are you here as J's chaperone?"

"Well, we're here together but I'm actually going to be singing."

"I didn't see your name on the gospel schedule."

"I'm replacing Gladys Knight."

"For the rhythm and blues concert?"

"Yes."

"Oh," says Eugenia, her tone changing drastically. "I thought you gave up that life years ago."

"What do you mean by 'that life'?" I want to ask. *"Do you presume all R&B singers have low or no morals? By 'that life' are you saying I was a drug addict or a drunk? Exactly what do you mean by 'that life'? And what gives you the right to address me in such an accusatory way?"* But I try not to be defensive in my reply.

"Actually," I say, "I loved that life. I found it rewarding and creative."

"Then why did you leave it?"

"A higher calling."

"And now the lower calling is luring you back?"

Lord, have mercy! I think to myself, this woman is trying to push my buttons. Why? Is she antagonistic because J won't sign up with her management company?

"I don't feel lured back. I feel honored being asked to replace a great artist like Gladys."

"There won't be any of those gangsta rappers on the bill, will there?" Eugenia asks.

"I don't think so."

"I find them so vulgar, so detrimental to the moral development of our youth. If only rap music would be restricted to the sort of songs J performs. Wouldn't that be wonderful, Albertina?"

"Yes, it would."

"So you'll be sure to keep him from that life, won't you, Pastor?"

There's that phrase again. *That life.* Does Bishop's wife think I'm luring my godson into a life of debauchery? Surely she knows me better than that. Then why would she even say such a thing? And why am I so concerned with her misperceptions of me?

"I must help my husband prepare for his presentation," she says. "He and four other prominent preachers will be speaking in a few hours. I hope you can break away from the dance crowd long enough to come hear him."

"I'll try my best, Eugenia," I say before going on my way, puzzled and a bit hurt.

By Saturday morning, I'm over the hurt. I have to be because it's time to rehearse. I know the musicians who are backing me. The keyboardist is my good friend Booker T. Jones, who gained fame with his hit-making group, Booker T. and the MGs.

The rehearsal goes smoothly. The guys know my material better than I do. They play the arrangements flawlessly and, even more to the point, soulfully. I'm relaxed and grateful.

That afternoon I go back to the hotel to relax and pray. I've been given a three-bedroom suite. Justine, in from Hawaii, and my hairdresser, Blondie, share one room, I have another, and J has the third.

"There are so many old battle-axes standing guard over this poor boy," says Justine, "that no young girl has a chance."

"I'm glad," I say. "I just want him to concentrate on his performance at the gospel concert Sunday."

My concert starts at eight and, I confess, I'm a little nervous. After all, it's been a while. I start getting ready at about five. I want to give Blondie all the time she needs. I also want to give Justine time to press my gown and help me pick out the accessories. The gown is green satin and the accessories are strands of pearls, a small gold watch, and the most precious piece of jewelry I own, my mother's engagement ring, a small emerald-cut diamond.

Blondie and Justine do their jobs beautifully. I'm blessed to have them surrounding me at this new, yet old moment in my life. I've sung the blues before, of course, but not as the solo star in a venue of this magnitude. For a split second, I wonder if I'll rise to the occasion. I wonder if the fear factor will overtake me. But when that happens, I turn to God. Before we leave for the venue, I ask Justine and Blondie if we can join hands. I say, "Father, I just want to stop and offer up to You all my little butter-flies, all my little fears, all my little apprehensions about going out and singing for so many people. I just want to stop and pray that everyone who hears me tonight is blessed by Your grace and guiding light. Let them see You in me, Father, let them feel the joy that is Jesus and the energy that is Your sweet music. Let me perform for Your glory, Your goodness, Your everlasting love. In Jesus' name, Amen."

At that moment, the door to the suite opens and J, accompanied by Damitra, walks in.

"We were just praying, children," I say.

"We've been praying all day with the gospel stars," says Damitra. Her comment sounds snide, but maybe I'm misinterpreting her tone; maybe I'm confusing her with her mother.

"My parents gave me permission to come to the concert with J tonight, but they won't be coming," she adds.

Why tell me that?

"Well, dear," I say, "I hope you enjoy it."

"I can't wait, Aunt T," says J. "I know you're going to turn it out."

"Thank you, sweetheart. I'm going to try."

In truth, I don't try. I relax. When my name is announced and I walk out on stage to a thunderous ovation, when I look out at that huge crowd, I can't help but relax. Love will do that to you. Yes, I feel love, and it's love that lets you relax. Love lets you know you're already accepted. Love is the greatest relaxant I know of. And believe you me, this starry night in Atlanta, I have never felt more relaxed or loved in my life.

I haven't realized how the fans have missed me. I thought they'd forgotten me. But they haven't. Given their enthusiasm, I figure I better start off with a bang. No time to mess around. Get right to it.

"Thank you very much," I tell the audience, "and God bless every one of you. Here's the little tune that, back in the day, put me on the map. I hope you still remember it."

And with that, I jump right into my signature song, "Sanctified Blues."

> *Moon is howling outside my window*
> *Wind is crying and I'm staring at the phone*
> *Mama said, "There'll be nights like this, child,*
> *When a man loves you, then leaves you all alone."*
>
> *Got the sanctified blues . . .*
> *I miss the church where Mama raised me*
>
> *Got those sanctified blues . . .*
> *Miss the wisdom that Mama gave me*
>
> *Sanctified blues . . .*
> *This man ain't what he said*
>
> *Sanctified blues . . .*
> *Said he was a saint, then led me to his bed*
>
> *When that church got to shoutin'*
> *And the Holy Ghost ran up and down the pews*
> *I saw this man with pretty brown eyes*
> *Saying, "Girl, let me spread the good news."*
>
> *Sanctified blues . . .*
> *Oh, he looked so fine, his words were strong and true*

Sanctified blues . . .
Lord, have mercy—if only I knew

The audience goes crazy and makes me sing it again! I'm only too happy to oblige. From there I sing my second number one hit, "Stay Out of the Kitchen," before doing a medley of Otis Redding songs, everything from "Mr. Pitiful" to "Dock of the Bay." "Your Good Thing's About to Come to an End" precedes "Action Speaks Louder Than Words." The more I sing, the stronger my voice becomes. I know it's not me—I've had throat problems in the past—it's God. God is inside every song I'm singing and God is pushing me to my potential. I'm singing three, four, five more songs than I had planned. And the audience is loving it.

When I know I have to quit, I say, "This is more than I've ever dreamed of. And because, in addition to being a singer, I'm also a minister, I'd like to have a little church here. I'm not talking about preaching or passing the basket, I'm just talking about stopping to acknowledge His presence, right here and right now."

When I sing the great gospel number "Mary, Don't You Weep," the crowd sings along with me. We have church.

"Thank you, Jesus!" I say before leaving the stage. "Never stop loving Him, never stop giving Him the praise!"

A cry of "Amen" rises up and fills the Georgia Superdome.

In the wings, Justine and Blondie give me huge hugs.

"You done it, baby," says Justine. "You threw down."

"I was lucky I didn't throw up," I confess.

"Well, you didn't look nervous," says Blondie. "You looked wonderful."

After the concert there's a reception where I see dozens of old friends. They regale me with congratulations. I look around for J and Damitra, but they're nowhere to be found.

Back at the suite, it's one a.m. Blondie and Justine have both retired. I can't keep my eyes open. The door to J's room is closed. He's left a note for me on the coffee table.

"You did great, Aunt T! I'm proud! My godmother is a super-star!"

The late edition of the *Atlanta Journal-Constitution* says the same thing: "The highlight of this year's African American music celebration so far was the surprise appearance of Albertina Merci. Now an ordained preacher, Miss Merci returned to form as a secular superstar. She had the crowd on its feet for her hourlong set and, if we're lucky, we'll remember last night's performance as the moment a legendary singer reclaimed her throne as one of the queens of rhythm and blues."

Justine and Blondie are ecstatic about the notice, and of course I couldn't be more pleased. With God's help, I was able to give the fans what they wanted. Thank you, Jesus.

By nine a.m., though, J still hasn't emerged from his room. His own gospel performance this morning begins at eleven, so I gently knock on his door. I think I hear more than one voice in there, and I grow alarmed. Did he dare bring Damitra to his room last night? I can't believe he'd do such a thing, but my imagination starts to race. I knock a little louder. This time he opens the door. He's bleary-eyed, and the radio is playing. The other voice was coming from the radio. J is alone. Thank you, Jesus.

"I was just getting up, Aunt T. I need to hustle and get over to the Superdome. You and your posse are coming with me, aren't you?"

My posse consists of Justine and Blondie.

"Of course," I say. "We wouldn't miss it for the world."

arvin Winans, Donnie McClurkin, Kirk Franklin, Mary Mary, Fred Hammond, Smokie Norful, Hezekiah Walker— the lineup for the gospel show is spectacular. The performances are brilliant, but no one moves the young audience like J. After his first two numbers, he comes to the mic and says, "This next song is for someone who's been there in my time of need. Many of you saw her last night, so you know what I'm talking about when I say she's sensational. She's my godmother, and a blessing in my life. I'd like to ask Pastor Albertina Merci to stand up as I get my praise on in her honor. I call this one 'Angel Aunt.'"

J launches into the rap he wrote for me. The crowd eats it up, and by the time he hits the hook, everyone's up and dancing.

> *No matter how bad*
> *Negativity attacks*
> *You can be sure*
> *God's got your back*
> *Say, no matter how bad*
> *Negativity attacks*
> *You can be sure*
> *God's got your back.*

At the postconcert party, Eugenia Gold is the first to come up to me.

"Paster Merci," she says, "I see you've returned to your first love. I congratulate you on your new career. Will you be giving up your church to pursue the blues full-time?"

What is it with this woman?

"Certainly not," I say. "My commitment to my church is firm."

"When the offers start rolling in, that commitment might well be tested."

Other than the difficult encounter with Bishop's wife, the party is fun. I see people I haven't seen in years. I'm congratulated on last night's performance and I'm congratulated on being the subject of J's heartfelt rap.

J is at the party, of course, and Damitra is on his arm.

"Thank you for that beautiful gift," I tell him. "Your dedication meant so much to me."

"Anything for my Aunt T," he says.

"It's been a big weekend, J," I say. "But all good things come to an end. We're booked on the red-eye tonight so you can get to school tomorrow morning."

"Actually, if you don't mind, Aunt T, I'll be going back earlier on Bishop's private jet. They're flying to L.A. to drop off Damitra, and they have one extra space. We'll arrive around ten p.m. That way I'll get a good night's rest."

Before I have a chance to react, J and Damitra are whisked away to do a joint interview with a gospel magazine.

"How does it feel to be a role model for Christian young people?" asks the reporter.

"I try my best to live up to that role," says J.

"There must be a great deal of pressure," the reporter observes.

"No one handles the pressure better than J," says Damitra. "But to his female fans out there I just want to say, 'Hands off, girls. He's all mine.'"

And with a wink and a smile, Damitra gives J an innocent kiss on the cheek.

Parker, Mint Management

I can take you where you want to go, Albertina."

"I don't want to go anywhere, Parker," I say. "I'm doing just fine with my life and my church. I'm not about to leave my church."

"You're the one who always says that you take your church with you. You carry your church in your heart. That's a direct quote from Pastor Albertina Merci."

It's late September and Parker has flown to L.A. to convince me to take a string of dates on B.B. King's Holiday Blues Tour, starting up in November and going through New Year's.

"I have it worked out," he says, "where you'll miss only a few Sundays. The big holiday dates—Thanksgiving, Christmas, and New Year's—are Southern California venues, so you'll be right here. Couldn't be any more comfortable for you."

"I'm not sure, Parker."

"I am. And I'm sure of something else. A recording contract. When was the last time you cut a record?"

"It's been a while."

"Well, an A&R guy from Universal Music was at the Superdome. He was knocked out and asked for your number. He thinks an Albertina Merci comeback record will cause a sensation."

"Come back from where?" I ask.

"Come back from being missing in action."

"I've been in action," I say. "God's action."

"God knows your true talent is for entertaining people, Albertina. Don't tell me it didn't feel good out there with everyone going crazy for you."

"Sure it felt good. But I saw it as a one-time thing."

"I see it as the start of the biggest chapter of your career. And I'm here to convince you that Parker Mint Management will put you back on the map where you belong."

Parker Mint is a salesman. He's slick but he's also sincere. He has taste in music and he has worked with the best. Dark skinned, rail thin, expensively dressed, Rolex on one wrist, gold bracelet on the other, straight even teeth, narrow nose, high forehead, pretty green eyes—the man is hard to ignore. Mr. Mario, who is sitting in on this meeting, scrutinizes him carefully. When Parker is gone, Mario says, "I don't trust him."

"I do," I counter.

"Then why'd you turn down his offer?"

"I didn't," I say. "I just need time to think."

"So he got to you, is that it?"

"It isn't about him, Mario, it's about this tour with B.B. It might be something I'd enjoy."

"And what about leaving the church?" he asks.

"All of a sudden you're concerned about a church you never attend."

"I just don't want you to get hurt."

"How am I going to be hurt if I have a written contract to do a specified number of dates?"

"These slimy promoters can hurt anyone they want."

"And why would Parker want to hurt me? I've known the man for decades. Plus, I had him call Bob Blakey. Blakey says Parker's the best R&B booking agent in the country. According to Bob, the terms he offered were more than fair."

"Didn't you say he was a womanizer?"

"I said he has a way with women."

"First night you're out there, he'll be hitting on you."

"My Lord, Mario, you are actually jealous, aren't you?"

"No, just realistic."

"I'm flattered that you'd think Parker has romantic designs on me."

"I saw it in his eyes," says Mario. "He ain't about nothing but scoring with the ladies. He's all bull."

The phone interrupts us. It's Harry Weinger, a leading producer with Universal Music. He has produced many of the great Motown reissues and won a Grammy for his work with James Brown. He wants to sign me to a contract. He wants to get started helping me select songs and musicians. He's willing to fly in from New York to do the sessions in L.A. Anything to make me happy. He wants the name of my lawyer so contracts can be drawn up. I'm flabbergasted. Parker wasn't kidding. Out of nowhere, I'm in demand. I tell Harry to give me a few days and I'll get back to him. "Take all the time you need, Albertina," he says, "but please think long and hard about how much this record could mean to music lovers around the world."

I tell Mario about the discussion.

"Your recording doesn't bother me," he says, "but touring does. You'll be taking on too much. And you don't need to get involved with a sleazeball like Mint."

"Please, Mario, don't disparage people you don't know. I find that offensive."

"Sorry, Albertina, but you'll be walking into a den of wolves."

"I've had some experience in the R&B field before," I tell him. "I'm not exactly a babe in the woods."

"You're my babe," says Mario, "and if you're going to be walking through the woods, I'm going to be by your side."

I'm touched by his concern. I kiss his cheek and say, "Thank you, Mario. I know you care."

"More than you can imagine, Albertina."

I f Mario cared all that much, he'd join your church and make you an honest woman," Justine tells me when I report the day's events to her over the phone. She's calling from Hawaii.

"I think he does care," I say.

"He's a strange cat. He knows you'd marry him if he became a Christian but he's too damn stubborn to give up his nonbelieving ways."

"Stubbornness is something you can relate to, Justine."

"I relate big-time, but all I'm saying, Albertina, is that this is your chance to get back to the big time. I sure as hell wouldn't let any jealous man stand in your way. Besides, I like this Parker Mint. Fact is, I had dinner with him last night at the Mandarin Oriental Hotel in Kahala."

"You *what?*" I ask in astonishment.

"I had dinner with the man. Is that a crime?"

"What is Parker doing in Hawaii?"

"He's booking some acts for the Honolulu Bowl. When we

were in Atlanta, he mentioned he was coming, and I mentioned I lived here. That's all."

"Did your husband enjoy meeting him?" I ask.

"My husband is on Maui for a two-week engagement."

"Don't you think you should join him?"

"Albertina, my husband is a very liberal man. He knows I enjoy the company of other gentlemen, and he trusts me implicitly."

"Well, I'm glad to hear that you and Parker kept it all above board."

"I wouldn't go that far."

"Justine! Parker Mint is notorious."

"Same's been said about me," she says. "But whatever Parker may be, he's convinced he can put you back in the spotlight. And that's all I care about. You'll be living large, and I'll be living vicariously through you. What could be better for two old ladies like us?"

"I don't know what to say, Justine."

"Well, I do. Sign that contract Parker's about to send you. Sign it quick."

Two weeks later, I sign the contract. After many days of prayerful thought, I feel strongly that the Lord wants me to sing.

I've worked out the schedule so I miss very few Sundays at House of Trust. Also, Naomi has been named associate pastor and has won over everyone's heart. She and Patrick have dedicated themselves completely to making sure that our church fulfills the needs of parishioners.

Meanwhile, I've arranged the dates for what will be my first secular release in decades. We'll be cutting the songs in the studios at the Capitol Tower in Hollywood, a landmark where, back in the fifties, Nat Cole invited me to watch one of his string sessions. I'm thrilled to be singing again. I'm feeling energy I haven't felt in years. I thank God for the opportunity, and I promise God that in this music my love for Him will be evident to all.

I'm also concentrating on my godson. I've curtailed his weekend concert dates and his weekend social dates. We've had some arguments about that, but I'm convinced that he has to slow down. He's doing well at the Crossroads School. He's especially popular among the girls and finds himself dating several at once.

"The girls don't mind sharing you?" I ask him.

"They don't seem to. Even when I tell them they're not the only one, they still don't mind. Only Damitra gets upset, but her dad moved her back to Dallas, so I haven't seen her that much."

"Why did Bishop do that?"

"For the same reason you watch *my* comings and goings, Aunt T. He thinks she's too wild."

"And is she, son?"

"I like Damitra. She's fun, and she's a superbad singer. She can praise the Lord with more sex appeal than anyone I know."

"I'm not sure that's a good thing."

"The gospel promoters think it is. She's offered more work than me. She's going to be singing in Madison Square Garden in a few weeks."

"Well, coincidentally, so am I."

"For the Music Mega Fest?"

"The same. If you'd like to join me for that weekend, I'd love to have you, J."

"I'd love it, Aunt T. They booked Deitrick Haddon with Damitra instead of me. I don't know why, but now it won't make any difference 'cause I'll get to go anyway."

"Long as I can keep track of your comings and goings."

"No doubt, Aunt T. No doubt."

Before the trip to New York, I go to Capitol Towers for one of the most satisfying recording sessions of my life. We take it all the way back and record live. While the musicians are playing, I'm singing. And the songs—"People Get Ready," "Love and Happiness," "How Sweet It Is," "You're All I Need to Get By," and one of my old compositions, "Love Tornado"—flow so smoothly everyone is smiling and calling for more. We finish up twelve tunes in four days.

"What are we going to call the album?" asks Harry Weinger, who's producing it.

"Gotta call it *Love Tornado*."

"That feels right to me," says Harry.

"Aunt T, Meet Uncle G"

It happens in mid-October in the lobby of the Four Seasons Hotel just off Park Avenue in New York City.

J introduces me to his uncle, his father's brother.

"I've always loved me some Albertina Merci," says Gates Turner, who resembles the late blues singer Jimmy Rushing, aka "Mister Five by Five." Gates is short and fat. His neck is hardly visible. He wears a ring on every finger except his thumbs—sapphires, diamonds, and emeralds. He wears gaudy diamond earrings and his floor-length overcoat is white mink. His mink hat matches his overcoat. His shoes are gleaming red alligators. From head to toe, the man is macked-out.

"It's been years, Mr. Turner," I say.

"Call me Gates. I was Gates to you before and I'm Gates to you now. I'm a fan, Albertina, I'm a fan of yours and a fan of my nephew here. He says you been taking mighty good care of him, and I gotta thank you for that. The Lord has blessed this boy."

"He certainly has," I agree.

"And the Lord has blessed me by letting me run into my old running buddy Parker Mint. He told me that you and J were up in this hotel. Thought I could take you both out for a big steak dinner. How's that sound to you, baby?"

"I need to rest tonight, Gates," I say. "Tomorrow's the concert. But feel free to take your nephew out. Long as you have him back by midnight."

"Well before that, ma'am," says Gates. First it was "baby," now it's "ma'am." Gates is giving me mixed messages. Which is perhaps why I'm feeling confused. Better to take off and leave J with his uncle.

Up in my room, I decide to call Parker Mint, who's staying across town at the Ritz-Carlton.

"You situated all right?" he asks.

"I'm fine, Parker. The two-bedroom suite you booked for me and J is perfect. Thank you."

"It's my pleasure, Albertina. Rehearsal tomorrow at noon. B.B. will be arriving at one. He's eager to see you."

"And I'm eager to see him, Parker. There's just one thing I wanna ask you."

"What's that?"

"What's your opinion of Gates Turner?"

A silence—a long, deadly silence—follows.

"Why you asking?"

"He's my godson's uncle."

"Keep him away from your godson."

"Why do you say that?"

"He's dangerous."

"In what way?" I ask, my heart beating fast.

"As you know, he started off as a fight promoter. Then he became a kingpin in the gangsta rap business until he got caught."

"Remind me what the charges were."

"Caught for financing his record company with drug money. He served time, you know. Served a couple of years."

"Have you done business with him?"

"I wouldn't touch him with a ten-foot pole. But I will say this. He ain't dumb. He's got a brilliant business mind, and, as far as the rapping game goes, no one's made more money. Just make sure he keeps his hands off J."

"He's with J now."

"You're gonna have to stay close to that kid, Albertina. The temptations for a talented young guy like that are overwhelming. But with your help, I don't see J being overwhelmed. Besides, he's a good Christian boy and a true believer."

"I believe that, Parker, but I'm still concerned."

"You're the one who always says that nothing or no one is stronger than God."

"But I never underestimate the damage the enemy can do."

"Well, I gotta say, Albertina, that Gates Turner is sure enough capable of doing some serious damage."

"I need to do some serious praying."

"Talking about prayer," says Parker, "your friend Justine is the answer to a longtime prayer of mine. Did she mention that we got together in Hawaii?"

"She did."

"Wonderful gal."

"Has a wonderful husband too."

"I know they're having their problems."

"Why do you say that, Parker?"

"I don't say it, she does. I don't think she's happy being stuck out there on an island in the middle of the Pacific."

"They call it paradise."

"Well," says Parker, "she's calling me all the time wanting to know if I could use a full-time wardrobe designer for my shows. Fact is, she wanted to come in to New York this weekend to help you out."

"I know. I told her it wasn't necessary."

"I told her to meet us in San Francisco in two weeks when we play the Fillmore. Which reminds me, Albertina, I've gotten a call for you to play a corporate gig down in Oakland. The Association of African American Bankers is having their national convention and they want you to entertain. You won't believe the fee."

"Let's talk about it later, Parker. Right now I'm going to try and sleep."

But sleep still doesn't come. I'm tossing and turning and feeling regret about having allowed J to go out with Gates when, sometime after eleven, I hear the door to the suite open. I put on a robe to see who's there.

J is in the living room, sitting on the couch, smiling.

"Hi, Aunt T."

I wonder if it's one of those high smiles induced by marijuana. Unlike Mario, I'm no expert at detecting subtle degrees of being high.

I sit on the couch next to him and ask, "Have a good time, honey?"

"Great time. Uncle G's a great guy."

"Is he?" I ask, sounding surprised.

"People misunderstand because he has a bad rep. And he's been given a bad rap, but when it comes to the streets, he's the real deal."

"And that's good?"

"At Crossroads, in that African American culture course I've been taking, we've been reading street literature. It's a whole category of books. There's one my teacher recommended called *Pimp,* by Iceberg Slim. It's considered a classic. It was written in the late sixties, Aunt T, but it's all about the ghetto in the forties and the fifties. Talk about keeping it real! When you read about that stuff in a book, it's exciting because you see how this guy influenced a whole generation that came after him. But when you meet a guy like that in person—and he turns out to be your uncle—man, you can't believe it. You can't stop listening to the stories."

"I can see why it'd be fascinating, but—"

"Uncle G also told me lots of stories about my dad that I didn't know. Turns out that in his day my dad Julius Turner was a bigger fight promoter than Don King. Julius was Gates's older brother and the reason Gates got into the promotion game. He told me how my dad was killed, and why, and he also told me the story of how he'd been framed."

"Your dad or Gates?"

"They both were framed."

"They got involved in a dangerous world," I say.

"But Uncle G survived. And now he's back. He's got one of the biggest management firms in show business. He has an amazing mind for business."

"I'm sure he does."

I don't want to denigrate the boy's uncle, a man I really don't know. That's not my place. But I do feel compelled to warn him. I do so gently. But despite my words, I can see that J's fascination with this man and what he represents—a hidden part of J's heritage—is far from abated. If anything, the more disparaging I am about the world of the Turner brothers, the more intriguing that world appears to my godson. In that world, bad is good and good is bad. Values are flipped and morality nonexistent. I decide to leave the topic of Uncle G alone, at least for the time being. My hope is that J's interest in that shady world will eventually dissipate.

"Uncle G's coming to your concert tomorrow night, Aunt T," J tells me before he goes off to bed. "He loves your singing. He's bringing a party of thirty or forty people. He bought out the first two rows."

The next night I'm onstage at Madison Square Garden and look down at the first two rows. Gates and his party people are having a fine time. They're up and dancing. They're cheering me on. They're singing the lyrics to my songs along with me. They're handing me a bouquet of two dozen roses. They're calling for encore after encore. And in their midst, seated next to Damitra Gold, is my godson, applauding and calling my name.

At the end of my set, when I decide to close with "Amazing Grace," I ask the audience to pray with me. The first rows are quick to get on their feet and hold each other's hands. "Thank you, Father, for the gift of music and its power to excite us with Your love. May that love lead us all into the life that honors You. In Jesus' name, Amen."

When I'm through singing "Amazing Grace," I walk to the edge of the stage. I extend my arms to the crowd, take a deep bow, and say, over and over again, "God bless you! God bless you all!" The house lights go up and I look down at the first two rows, where the party people are screaming the loudest. I see them waving and blowing me kisses. I also see Gates passing an overstuffed funny-looking cigarette to his lady friend. I doubt it's the kind that Marlboro makes.

ALIENATION OF AFFECTIONS

IT'S A FRIVOLOUS LAWSUIT," Bob Blakey tells me.

I've just faxed him the papers I've been served from Bishop and Eugenia Somerset Gold. The couple has sued me for alienating the affection of their daughter Damitra. They blame me for causing a break in their relationship with her. The complaint alleges that, because of my antagonism toward Bishop and his church, I convinced my godson to seduce Damitra, who, in turn, was convinced by my godson's uncle, Gates Turner, to leave their church and become a secular singer under his management.

It's quite a mess.

"They're desperate," says Bob, "and confused. We'll get a summary judgment within weeks and the suit will disappear."

All this is happening as I approach the holiday season, the busiest time of year for me. Not only are there dozens of church activities, but our big effort to feed the hungry and homeless kicks into high gear between Thanksgiving and Christmas. This year, because I have agreed to do a select number of bookings on B.B. King's tour, I am especially busy. Patrick and Naomi keep saying how they can handle it all. I have no reason not to believe them because they've been covering all the bases for me since J arrived. At the same time, I love my church responsibilities and miss performing them.

Now I'm facing my responsibility to J in regard to Damitra. Naturally I knew about her defection. J told me a week ago. And naturally I was shocked.

"Her parents must be furious," I said.

"They've disowned her," J told me. "But she doesn't care. She thinks they're too controlling."

"Is this something you and she discussed?" I asked J.

"She's always wanted to be a pop star, she always talked about it."

"And your uncle encouraged her."

"He paid her. He paid her a huge advance so she doesn't have to be dependent on her mom and dad. She's really got guts. She reminds me of you, Aunt T."

"Me?"

"Well, my mom told me how you went out there as a young girl to sing the blues. You were on your own, weren't you?"

"That was a different time, J."

"And now you're singing the blues again. I've seen the way Bishop and his wife and people from the church have been attacking you. But I've always been believing when you say it's all God's music and it's all good."

"Where is Damitra now?"

"She's moving to New York. Uncle G's relocating there too. He bought a brownstone in Brooklyn with a recording studio in the basement. He wants me to fly in to see it."

"That won't be happening anytime soon," I say.

"Why not?"

"School."

"I've made an A on every English and history paper. Got a B in math and B-plus in science. Isn't that good?"

"That's great," I say, "but you need to keep it up."

"Uncle G will send me a ticket. I'll leave Friday and be back Sunday. I'll only miss one day of school."

"Not a good idea, J."

"How come?"

"We'll talk about it later."

"What should I tell Uncle Gates?"

"Thank him for his generosity. But now is not the right time to visit him."

That night I discuss the dilemma with Mr. Mario.

"You think Gates Turner is pulling J into his stable?" he asks.

"Of course," I say. "It's obvious. He gets Damitra and Damitra will get J. He'll get him to give up his Christian market. He'll lure him with money and God knows what else."

There is a long silence on the other end of the line.

"I'd let him go to Brooklyn," says Mario.

"So I should just let him walk into the arms of the devil?"

"Isn't that what you did with Parker Mint?"

"Mario!" I say in exasperation. "Parker Mint is a legitimate, upstanding, well-regarded impresario. He books classic acts and runs a classy management firm. How can you compare him to Gates Turner, a convicted felon and someone interested in nothing but making money on gangsta rappers?"

"Parker Mint is interested in making money."

"Yes, but he's interested in the beauty and the dignity of the music. He's interested in keeping alive a great tradition."

"By now hip-hop has its own tradition. There's more to hip-hop than gangsta rap, Albertina. It's an art form."

"I have nothing against hip-hop, Mario. I am merely concerned for the moral well-being of my godson. Not to mention his financial well-being. Gates Turner will rob him blind."

"Look, Albertina, I have no illusions about this Turner character. I see him as a pimp. But I also don't see how you can lock J in his room for the next three years. He's going to do what he's going to do."

"Will you at least talk to him?" I ask.

"Are you admitting that he needs someone in his life to tell him what it means to be a man?"

"I've never thought otherwise, Mario," I say. "Please talk to him."

"My Flesh and Blood"

The next night Mario invites J to Stay Out of the Kitchen for dinner. J likes Mario. He likes hearing stories of Mario's heyday as a major actor on network television. He's impressed by Mario's knowledge of so many fields—health, food, jazz, sports, and the works of William Shakespeare.

I'm not there, but when I ask Mario about the encounter, he gives me a blow-by-blow report:

"Look here, son," Mario tells J, "you may be fascinated by your uncle, but he is not a course in exotic ghetto literature. This cat is real, and he's really dangerous."

"Not to me," says J.

"Son," Mario says, "you got a lot to learn about the business of being a man."

"Uncle G is the kind of man you'd like, Mr. Mario," says J. "I really think you would. He's all macked-out, but that's just on the outside. On the inside he's all heart. He's been through some stuff, and he's survived it all. He knew Tupac and Biggie, he knew 'em all. He can tell you why and how they were killed. He was there, right there on the front lines."

"And you think it's cool that he'll turn Damitra into Lil' Kim?"

"No, he's modeling her after Diana Ross. First hit songs, then hit movies. But it's going to be classy. He has a vision."

"And you've bought it, hook, line, and sinker."

"I haven't bought anything, Mr. Mario. He's never asked me to stop doing Christian rap. He admires that."

"And you don't think he's not going to eventually ask you?"

"Maybe, maybe not. Maybe I'm getting a message to him that no one else ever has. Ever think of it that way?"

"I think you're dreaming, J."

"Not long ago, Mr. Mario, you were telling me about how everyone thought the great blues singers, like Bessie Smith and Ma Rainey, were too raunchy. Then in my jazz course at Crossroads, I'm learning how when bebop came out in the forties, everyone was saying it was too radical, too angry. Beboppers were looked on like they were Martians. Isn't that right?"

"But beboppers weren't spitting pornography," says Mario.

"What about Henry Miller?"

"He was a great writer. Are you reading Henry Miller at school?"

"Didn't they call it pornography when it first came out?"

"Are you going to compare Henry Miller to Snoop Dogg?"

"Maybe," says J. "Maybe that would be a good essay for my English class."

"Son," says Mario, "I understand the inclination to romanticize literature and life. Believe me, I did it myself when I was a young man. But things are different these days. Gangsters have moved into the business in a way that's never been done before."

"You mean, Mr. Mario, that black artists haven't been cheated before? They didn't have their royalties ripped off in the fifties and sixties and even the seventies and eighties?"

"I'm not saying that, J. All I'm saying is that Gates Turner is notorious. And if you knew what was good for you, you'd stay away from him."

"He's my flesh and blood. He's my only link to my dad."

"He could also be the link to ruining your life. I can't be any plainer than that. The man's poison."

"And you have proof, Mr. Mario?"

"He has a history. He has a record. A jail record."

"So did Martin Luther King."

"Oh come on, J! You're not thinking clearly and you're not taking this thing seriously."

"Well, like you once said, Mr. Mario, 'A man's gotta do what he's gotta do.' "

After Mario reports the conversation to me, I'm alarmed.

"Seems like you made no headway," I say.

"I tried, Albertina, but the boy sees his uncle as some kind of Robin Hood figure. A good-guy outlaw."

"What can we do?"

"I'm afraid you're going to have to let him discover the truth for himself," said Mario. "Painful as that might be."

"I need to protect him. For Shaleena's sake. For his sake. For God's sake."

"What are your options? Military school? I don't think so."

"Prayer."

"Prayer may be your *only* option."

"Prayer is always the best option."

"Then go on and pray," Mario urges.

"You don't object? You've never encouraged me to pray. We've never prayed together."

"First time for everything."

"Father God," I pray, "we invoke Your holy Spirit and Your divine strength. We raise up my godson to You and ask that You protect him from all harm. We ask that he feel Your mighty comfort wherever he goes, and that Your angels carry him on their wings. May his eyes be open to Your truth, may Your truth direct his path. Father, give us wisdom to deal with this young man so that he responds in a positive way to our concern for his welfare. Help us navigate these tricky waters, Father. Teach us to nurture J so that he may grow up in Christ Jesus, ever more faithful and devoted to Your will. In Jesus' name, Amen."

"Amen," says Mario.

Next morning I'm talking to Bob Blakey about this lawsuit.

"Will it be reported on the news?" I ask.

"I'm afraid it's already circulating on the Internet," Bob says. "I think that's their purpose."

"They think that will bring their daughter back."

"They want to expose Gates Turner. And they're sure that J and you are part of the conspiracy to take Damitra away from them."

"That's crazy."

"They're enraged, and rage makes people do crazy things."

"I don't care what the public says about me," I tell Bob, "but I worry about the effect it will have on J."

"Have you told him about the suit?"

"I need to do so, especially if it's already on the Internet."

"Where is he?"

"He's due home from school any minute. He's also due to spend the Christmas holidays with his uncle in New York."

"You're going to allow that?"

"I don't want to, but neither do I want to give him something to react against."

"Can you go to New York with him, Albertina?"

"Perhaps I can squeeze in a few days."

"At this critical juncture," says Bob, "I know you want to keep a close eye on him. That may be the only way."

A half hour later, J arrives home. In his baggy jeans and oversized white T-shirt displaying a photo of the socially conscious rapper called Common, he greets me with a big hug.

"Got an A on my English paper," he says.

"That's wonderful, baby. What was it about?"

"Tupac. I wrote about his poetry and his acting career."

I think about Tupac's violent death, and the confusion he must have fought his entire life.

"He was a genius," says J. "Genius writer and genius actor."

"I know he means a lot to you."

"He means a lot to the world. Kids in Africa know about Tupac. Kids in Brazil and Japan. Plus, he's a great creative influence on high-consciousness rappers like Talib Kweli, Iriz, Krs-One, M1, and Outkast. Those guys are brilliant."

"You are brilliant as well, baby."

"Not like them."

"You have your own brilliance."

"Thanks, Aunt T, but you look like you wanna tell me something."

"I do, sweetheart," I say. "There's something we need to discuss."

"About the Golds suing you?"

"Yes. I'm so sorry, dear, that this is happening."

"Damitra thinks it's funny. She thinks her folks are crazy."

"They're just worried."

"They think they can control her," says J, "but I know her better. No one can control that girl. She's got her own mind and now she wants her own career. I admire her, Aunt T. I gave her lots of props for taking on her mom and dad. They ain't exactly lightweights."

"Well, this lawsuit . . ."

"It ain't about nothing, Aunt T. Just their way of being mean to you. I just talked to Bob Blakey on the cell. He told me what he told you—a judge is going to look at this and laugh."

"Well, I'm not just happy, J, being in the middle of the dispute between a daughter and her folks."

"You didn't do anything, Aunt T. They're scapegoating you. They're badmouthing you 'cause they don't know what else to do. But in a funny way, they're helping Damitra. It's just gonna keep causing more and more publicity that will help her career blow up. I think Uncle G's gotta be grinning from ear to ear. Uncle G's kicked back and cool. He's been planning Damitra's next move, and now it looks like Bishop made the move for him. Isn't that something?"

"It sure is something, J, but I can't say for sure what that 'something' is."

"I'll know more when I get to New York next week," he says.

"Talking about that trip, baby, I was thinking about going along with you."

"Wow! That'd be great. I'm proud of you. You're the woman with the courage to take on the church."

"Baby, I'm not exactly taking on any church. I have a church, and I love it."

"Maybe not the church, Aunt T, but the church members who condemn you. People like Bishop and his wife who think you've sold out 'cause you're singing the blues again. What got them so bad was when Damitra said, 'If J's aunt can do it and stay in God's grace, I can too.' That's when she told them she was going pop. And that's when they flipped."

I sigh.

This isn't the story I envisioned, but it sure is the story of living.

"Can we pray, J?" I ask my godson.

"Always, Aunt T."

"Father God, thank You for giving us this life. The twists and turns aren't always what we expect, but we know that, in every twist and every turn, You are with us. So let us breathe in Your presence and allow You to direct our lives. In Jesus' precious name, Amen."

"Amen," says J.

LiViNG LaRGE

The words "The Crib" are written on a gold plaque outside a brownstone in the high-class Park Slope section of Brooklyn. J and I have arrived. The man who has picked us up in the limo from the airport, Gates Turner's personal driver, carries our luggage and escorts us to the door. During the ride over he told us that Mr. Turner is paying his tuition so that he can complete his degree in business administration from Brooklyn College. "Mr. Turner," says the driver, "is a wonderful employer."

From the doorstep, I see the small white camera surveying us. Standing there, I expect a skimpily clad gal in a French maid's outfit to open the door. Instead, a tall distinguished-looking black woman wearing a tweed suit stands before us.

"I'm Beatrice Gray," she says in extremely proper English, "Damitra's tutor. I'm happy to meet you, Pastor Merci. This must be your godson."

"That's me," says J. "Is Damitra around?"

"She is. We'll be through with our literature lesson in about an hour. Meanwhile, Mr. Turner asked that you wait for him. Let me show you to his study. Then I must get back to Damitra. She'll be glad to know that you both are here."

The central color motif for The Crib is gold. There are paintings on the walls of Venetian landscapes and flying dolphins are framed in gold. The elaborate circular staircase just beyond the entryway has banisters painted in gold. A huge glittering gold chandelier hangs from the ceiling. The plush wall-to-wall carpet that covers every room has a golden hue, the same color as the walls. In the study there are gold crushed velvet couches and a big portrait of Gates Turner wearing a gold lamé suit. He's smiling in the portrait and looks more like a teddy bear than a promoter.

When he walks into the room, he's wearing a Ralph Lauren warmup suit with the Polo logo on the front of his hooded top. His shoes are gold-colored Adidas high-tops. He embraces his nephew warmly, and kisses me on the cheek.

"This is an honor, Pastor," he says. "My home is your home. There are two guest bedrooms on the third floor, and they're both reserved for you and J. The cook's off today, but she's back early tomorrow morning, and you'll tell her whatever you want to eat. Meanwhile, I've ordered pizza. Hope you like pizza, Pastor."

"Pizza's great," I say.

"The Crib is amazing," says J. "I've never seen any place like this."

"Wanna show you the game room, J. Pool table was custom built in Modena, Italy, same place they make sports cars. The screening room's in the basement. Two rows of theater-styled seats. Seventy-two-inch screen. Got me a library of four thousand flicks. Wait till you the see the music DVDs, Pastor. I got you singing at the WattsStax Music Festival from '72. You, Isaac Hayes, the Staple Singers, Albert King—man, you guys turned it out that day!"

My mind goes back to 1972. Happy memories. But my mind quickly returns to the man standing in front of us. Gates Turner, with his oversized Gucci sunglasses, is beaming with pride. He's thrilled to have us in his home. All that's clear. But what's not clear is how he accumulated this wealth. And as though he heard the silent question in my mind, he starts talking about that very subject.

He pops open a Red Bull energy drink and takes a big slug. He offers us a drink. I take water and J takes a Pepsi. "It's amazing when I look around this place and think that this time last year I was behind bars. Ain't it funny how things turn around? But to tell you the truth, when they locked me up, they didn't lock up my mind and didn't lock up my investments. See, I had my investments—all legit, one hundred percent legit—and my investments never stopped working for me. Truth be told, people, I made more money when I was away than when I was out here running the streets."

"What kind of investments, Uncle G?" asks J.

"Internet. I saw it coming when no one else did. I studied the stuff. Search engines. Yahoo. Google. Bought 'em early and held my holdings. Also real estate. Always big in real estate. Residential, commercial—you name it. I'm diversified. Gotta be diversified. Can't put all your eggs in one basket, can you, Pastor?"

"Looks like you've done well, Gates."

"I study the economy. Got me some economic advisers, just like the president of the United States. Got me a board of directors. Gates Turner, Inc. ain't no joke. The directors are respectable cats from respectable corporations. They respect me 'cause I came up from nothing."

I want to ask why, if all these investments were accruing income when he was in jail, did he have to borrow money from Shaleena when he was released? The question, though, would appear hostile. And what's the point of sounding hostile? My suspicion is that his money is drug related, but I have no proof or reason to confront him. Best just to go with the flow of the upcoming weekend.

"Thing is," says Gates, continuing his monologue, "I've also been studying the way our people buy their music. That's why I've gotten deep into the R&B and rap market. The big white corporations been selling our music for decades, but they learned how to sell it from black men like Berry Gordy. Problem is, the black men who make it big wind up cashing out to the white corporations. Can't blame them, though, can we? They worked hard, started from scratch, and deserve whatever they can get. The pioneers are entitled to a big payday. They wanna live up in Bel Air or out there in Hawaii, that's fine. But me, I'm still on the streets 'cause the streets are changing every day and in every way. The groove is a beautiful thing, but the groove is about *now*, not yesterday. You know that, Pastor. You were there when Bo Diddley had the groove, and then it was Ike and Tina, and then it was James Brown, and Brother Ray had it before it moved to Otis and Isaac and Sly and Parliament and Funkadelic and Prince, before hip-hop popped up with Grandmaster Flash and the Furious Five and all them mighty cats that came afterward.

"See, I've studied my history. I know my history. I know my people's music. Which is another reason I'm so glad you've agreed to be my guest this weekend. It's surely a pleasure to see you, Pastor, but I also have business ideas for you. I love how you're back out there singing the blues, and I love how my friend Parker Mint has arranged good gigs for you. Beautiful. Just beautiful. But Gates Turner is always thinking. Gates Turner has the kind of mind that never stops. And ever since I been back with my nephew J and seen his talent, I've been thinking even more. I been thinking how you took care of this boy since the awful tragedy of my beloved sister-in-law. Been thinking, Pastor, that you showed this kid how God is working in his life. Beautiful. Just beautiful. God has chosen you to take care of this child, and I couldn't be happier. Gates Turner is a man of God. And God has also been leading me to see that the differences in our music are something we make up in our minds. Ain't no devil's music. It's all God's music. And you, Pastor, you are one of the people who showed me that. You said, 'I'll keep my church, but I'll go back and sing the blues. Ain't no sin in the blues.' Well, hallelujah, Pastor! Glory to God!"

Gates stops to take a breath and pop open another can of Red Bull. If I understand this man, this is the moment when he's going to give the argument for why J should leave gospel for gangsta rap.

"So here's what I'm thinking," Gates continues. "Thinking that sure, it's great that Parker Mint is booking you with B.B. King. Great that your old fans are getting to hear you again like they first heard you. But I gotta ask myself the question—is that really you? Is that how Pastor Albertina Merci feels about the world today? Or is that Albertina going back and remembering the way it used to be? Now don't get me wrong. Nostalgia is fine. Nostalgia is fun. And by the big crowds you've been attracting, there ain't no doubt that nostalgia is selling. The old music is good music. Old school ain't ever going outta style. Believe you me. Gates Turner is old school. But Gates Turner is also looking at the big picture. See, that's what's wrong with these promoters. The Parker Mints of this world are cool. But they thinking small. They thinking, how do I fill a two-thousand-seat arena? I'm thinking, how do I fill an eighty-thousand-seat stadium? And not just fill it with young people screaming for Usher or Chris Brown while their parents are home watching reruns of *Benson,* but fill it with families.

"It's the family that worries me, Pastor. The way the black family done broke down. That's the cause of all our problems. The family is the key. Strong family means the kids are in line. Broken family means the kids are running wild. That's it. So all this is a long-winded way of saying that I got a plan to keep those families together. I got a plan to promote entertainment that will attract the parents along with their kids. I look at you, Pastor, and I look at my nephew J, and I see a beautiful combination, a beautiful story of godmother and godson, different generations whose talents will definitely attract different members of the same family. No doubt about it. But to make it work, I'm gonna ask you to consider a compromise, Pastor."

Here it comes, I think to myself.

"I want you to return to your roots, Pastor," he says. "I want you to go back and sing gospel."

I'm stunned. I look over at J and see that he's smiling.

"What do you think, Aunt T?"

"I'm not sure I understand."

"A tour," says Gates. "Not just a tour, but *the* tour. The 'God Is the Good Groove' tour. The tour that's all gospel, all God. I want you and J to headline that tour. But it'll only happen, Pastor, if you're willing to give up your blues career and come back to Jesus."

"It's a slam dunk," says J.

I don't say anything. I'm too flabbergasted to respond. Gates Turner has taken me totally by surprise. Do I want to sing gospel? Of course I want to sing gospel. I began singing gospel. I started singing in church before I had ever heard the blues. I love gospel music and have planned to do a gospel album of my own. This opportunity through Parker Mint just happened by chance. It wasn't part of any plan, and, though I've loved those concerts and enjoyed the attention they have brought me, given a choice between gospel and blues, I'd choose gospel in a hot minute, especially gospel in conjunction with my godson.

It seems perfect.

It seems too perfect.

I don't want to be skeptical, but I have to be.

This is all too good.

Now here comes Damitra with her tutor, Beatrice Gray. I'm supposed to see that Damitra is dressed conservatively, a modest blue skirt, a white blouse, and a blue cardigan sweater. She looks like she might be attending a Catholic girls' school. She runs over and greets J with a hug, then comes and warmly kisses me on the cheek.

"Thank you, Pastor, for being such a wonderful role model," she says. "I couldn't make this change without you. And I'm sorry my parents are causing so much trouble, but they just don't understand."

What I don't understand is where Damitra is living.

"Beatrice runs a finishing school for girls over in Brooklyn Heights," says Gates. "She learned her skills from Maxine Powell, who started the charm school for Motown. Maxine was the one who gave the Supremes their class. But Beatrice also tutors the girls in reading and writing and all that grammar business. It's a boarding school and a charm school both. She's certified by the city. Damitra will get her high school degree right on time. Ain't no funny stuff over there. It's discipline, discipline, discipline. Beatrice done graduated a bunch of famous models, actresses, and singers. They come from as far away as Colorado and Florida. World-famous school. Hope you'll go by and check it out while you're here, Pastor. You can teach 'em about God. Everybody needs to know about God. Yes, sir, Gates Turner is all about doing everything for God."

"Gates Turner is a colossal fraud," says Mr. Mario when I call him that night before I go to sleep. The guest room, which is next to J's, is done up in turquoise-and-gold striped wallpaper. The décor makes me a little dizzy.

"I can't argue with you, Mario," I say, "but I can't prove it. He says he welcomes a call from Bob Blakey to go over the contracts he's offering me and J for a series of concerts. The guarantees are twice what Parker Mint is paying."

"He's tricking you," says Mario.

"How?"

"By giving you exactly what you didn't expect. You expected him to try to recruit J to do that crappy rap. Instead he's saying, 'Sing gospel, and do megaconcerts with your Christian godson.' He's playing into your weakness."

"Christianity is hardly my weakness."

"You understand what I mean."

"I don't. I have to take him at face value."

"Why?" asks Mario.

"Why not? If J and I get to spread the Word, then we'll be spreading the Word. Maybe he's turned a corner."

"And what about Damitra? You know he's turning her into Lil' Kim."

"Not by the look of things here," I say. "He's got her in a finishing school. He's looking after her schooling and seems to be doing a good job."

"Next you'll tell me, Albertina, that he found Jesus and is a God-fearing Christian."

"That's what he says."

"Save me from the Christians!" Mario shouts over the coast-to-coast long-distance line. "Now they've claimed the infamous Gates Turner!"

"All I'm claiming, Mario, is that he seems to be offering us something good."

"You'd do better to stick with Parker Mint. He'll rob you, but with less skill than Gates."

"You'd rather have me singing the blues than gospel, Mario. I realize that, and I understand why you'd feel that way."

"It's not that, Albertina. You're a great singer and could sing the Yellow Pages and make 'em sound beautiful. But these men are manipulating you."

"*These men?* You see it as a man/woman thing, Mario?"

"Definitely. You're naive."

"You're sounding accusatory, Mario."

"You sound like you're falling under the spell of a Svengali. He gets you, then he gets your godson. He already has the preacher's daughter. Don't you see the plan?"

In one way, I do see the plan. But I also have seen man's capacity for change. Is Gates Turner changing? And if he is, why should my inability to see that change get in the way? Maybe he has seen the light—or at least some kind of light. Dark prison days can do that to a man.

At any rate, the bottom line is that through all my days God is with me. God is leading me. And just as surely as He has led me to The Crib in Brooklyn, He will lead me to where I need to go and to what I need to do.

"Thank You, Jesus," I say before shutting my eyes and drifting off to sleep, with Mario's words of warning still ringing in my ear. "Thank You, Lord, for making life so interesting."

"An Absolute Tearjerker"

No OFFENSE," I tell the reporter from *Ebony* magazine, "but I'm not comfortable with the word 'tearjerker.' It implies some kind of sensationalism."

"Sorry, Pastor," says the young woman interviewing me, "I just mean the idea of how you were able to convert Gates Turner and, in turn, how he was able to reunite you and your godson to perform gospel concerts together."

"Well, the concerts aren't set yet and I'm not sure I participated in Mr. Turner's conversion"—*if there was one,* I want to add, but don't.

"The way he tells the story, you brought him to Christ. Once he got out of jail and found out that not only had his sister-in-law been killed in that horrible accident, but that you had adopted her son, he had to seek you out. He had to see who this God-loving person was. He credits you with his salvation, Pastor. How do you feel about that?"

"Anytime anyone is saved it's surely a blessing. To the extent that I carry Christ in my heart and allow Him to touch others, I rejoice. But I give Him all the glory. Like all of us, I'm just a broken vehicle. With Him, I'm whole."

"Amen, Pastor. But surely it must be a double blessing when a man with a past like Gates Turner not only comes into your life as a Christian, but becomes instrumental in helping you spread God's word."

How do I respond? If I say no, I sound blasphemous. If I say yes, I'm endorsing what sounds like Gates's public relations campaign to create an image of himself as an outstanding citizen. I feel foolish for having agreed to this interview, but on the other hand, when a national magazine calls and expresses interest in my ministry and the ministry of my godson, I'd feel even more foolish refusing to speak.

The problem is that the story is being spun, and there's nothing I can do about it. Gates is doing the spinning. His publicist contacted *Ebony*; his publicist told the magazine that I had become Gates's spiritual mentor; his publicist suggested the angle that would put Gates in the best possible light. The irony, of course, is that the article also puts me in a good light. So why complain? Why not take credit for bringing a man to the Lord? Because I didn't. Or I haven't. Or if I have, I can't be sure I have.

Right now I can't be sure about anything.

"Tell us a little about your own story, Pastor," asks the *Ebony* writer, helping me get beyond the issue of Gates. "Tell us how you made the transition from the secular to the sacred and back again. And then, if I understand, back a second time."

"The truth is that I never left the church because I carry the church in my heart. My folks were believers, I was brought up believing and have never *not* believed, not for a single second of a single day."

"Even when you were singing songs some considered nasty."

"Some might have seen them as nasty, but I never did. If I had, I wouldn't have sung them. You sing the songs that tell the story of your life as you're living your life. Your life changes, and so do the songs."

"Then why did you go back to singing the blues earlier this year?"

"Because I wanted to revisit an earlier part of my life. Nostalgia is a beautiful thing. It lets us reflect on where we've been and how we've grown. Reflection is a good thing. Reflection on God's goodness, on how He's taken us a mighty long way. There's no sin in reflection. There's no sin in going back and reliving memories that are sweet and moments that changed our direction."

"But now, according to Gates Turner, he has helped you find your way back to your true direction—gospel."

I want to be clear, I want to express my heart openly and lovingly, but I need God's help. I silently pray for the right words.

"Everyone I meet helps me find my true direction," I say, "because I look for Jesus in everyone I meet. When I see Him, He directs me. Some folk don't seem to have any Jesus in them, but everyone's capable of receiving Him. Jesus said, 'I stand at the door of your heart and knock.'"

"That's quite an answer," says the reporter.

"Well," I say, "that was quite a question."

The deeper question is always this: Have you lost your contact with God? And if you have, why? And how do you reconnect?

Because God lives inside, He can't go away. He said He would never leave me or forsake me. But our minds can drift and find

149

distractions. Mine certainly can. We can go to doubt. And we can go to fear. We can go to regretting the past. *Should I have agreed to come to New York with J? Was I right to stay with Gates Turner as his houseguest?* Or my mind can go to the fear of the future. *Will Gates Turner ruin my reputation as a pastor? Will he corrupt J?*

When this happens, like it is happening now as J and I fly back home to L.A., I try and gently remind myself that God lives in present tense only. When Moses asked Him to identify Himself, He said, "I am that I am." He didn't say, "I was" or "I will be." God exists now. And now is all we have. Now my nephew is sitting next to me reading *Vibe* magazine. Now I am looking out the window at the farmlands below. Now I am thinking of God's bounty, God's connections, God's presence in everything we do.

I am thinking that our trip to New York has happened, but that is the past. I learned many things. I encountered a man who is unquestionably brilliant in many ways. Gates Turner has been put in my life for a reason. The same goes for J. The same goes for everyone I encounter. God alone knows the reason. I am here to show how Christ lives within me. I show it when I sing, and I show it when I speak. I show it when I remain silent. I show it when, with God's help, I navigate my way through the twists and turns of the story I'm living. These days it feels like I'm living a soap opera. But aren't we all? Isn't that why soap operas are popular? They reflect the drama of our lives. I thank God for that drama, and even—or especially—for the challenge represented by Gates Turner.

Christmas is a calm time. J stays close to the house, attends church with me, and hangs out with his Crossroads friends at the mall. He and I and Mr. Mario spend Christmas day together. Mario gives me a box of Ella Fitzgerald CDs and gives J a rare copy of *The Autobiography of Malcolm X* signed by Malcolm's ghostwriter, Alex Haley. I give Mario jade cufflinks and J a gold cross. In turn, J gives me an exquisite cross carved from ivory.

Gates Turner sends a check for $100,000 designated for my church's "feed the hungry" drive.

J asks if he can give a New Year's party at our house. I'm happy to comply, but tell him that liquor or drugs won't be allowed.

"I realize that," he says. "I just want you to meet some of my friends. Damitra will also be flying in, but she'll be staying with her aunt. And of course Mr. Mario is welcome. Everyone wants to meet Mr. Mario."

His school friends are a mixed bunch—Jewish, African American, Latino, Korean, you name it. The boys are well mannered and the girls could not be nicer. They seem happy to drink punch and listen to my old-school records. Mr. Mario regales them with stories of TV shows from back in the day. He also provides a spread of healthy snacks. It all seems too good to be true.

Damitra arrives prim and proper. She doesn't look at all like Lil' Kim but more like a young Diahann Carroll. Gates is preparing her for a mainstream career in pop. "Nothing tawdry," he has told me. "Class all the way."

She speaks about the album they were recording in New York and the sounds she has chosen. "All that oversexed teen girl stuff is played out," she says. "Mr. Turner understands that young people need something wholesome."

At midnight, when the Times Square ball drops, we stand before the television cheering. Then J asks me to pray.

"Father God," I say, "thank You for bringing us together in fellowship and joy. Keep us present. Keep us ever mindful of

You. Keep us in the spirit of celebration, now and forever. In Jesus' name. Amen."

On January 2, the day Damitra is due to fly back to New York, she shows up at the house unexpectedly. J has just gotten home from school.

"I think I should tell you both," she says.

"What is it, honey?" I ask.

"I would have told you before, but I wanted us to enjoy the holidays. I have this problem that we need to discuss."

"What problem?" asks J.

"I'm pregnant with your child."

The Truth Is the Truth

When I listen to Marvin Gaye's immortal album *What's Going On*, the song that always stops me is "Save the Children." "Live life for the children," Marvin sings. It's the emotional highpoint of an emotional record that sounds better today than when Marvin made it nearly forty years ago.

I met Marvin fifty years ago. He was a drummer at Motown before he was a singer. A handsome guy with a sweet, winning manner, he had a shy cool that no one could resist. When he started to sing, and write songs as well, everyone in the business took note. He had his great R&B hits in the sixties, everything from "Pride and Joy" to "Heard It Through the Grapevine." But it wasn't until *What's Going On* that we realized that Marvin was a genius. And a preacher. Those songs were sermons. They invoked the spirit of a loving God who informed every note that Marvin sang. You couldn't call the record gospel, but the good Gospel of Jesus Christ was all over it. You couldn't call it blues, but it was as blue as it could be. What you could call it, though, was the truth.

The truth is the truth.

Marvin told the truth when he said, "Save the babies." Damitra told the truth when she said that she was pregnant. And my godson J told the truth when he said that yes, he and Damitra had been intimate several times and he was certain the baby was his.

"You won't like what I have to say," says Mario when I tell him the news.

"Then don't say it," I say.

"I'm not judging J and I'm not judging Damitra. Most teenagers don't have the restraint to resist their sexual urges. I know I didn't. So I'm not blaming anybody. I'm just saying that the presence of a child will only—"

"Stop yourself right there, Mario. You're wasting your breath."

"How old are they?" he asks.

"Damitra just turned eighteen, and J turns sixteen later this month."

"And you still think that they're old enough to care for—" says Mario.

"I think we need to save the babies, yes, I do," I insist.

"But who are the babies? Aren't Damitra and J babies having babies?"

"We need to save all the babies," I say. "Every single one of them."

"I can't talk to you about this, can I, Albertina?"

"No, you can't, Mario. When it comes to saving babies, there's no discussion."

ave you discussed this with your parents?" I ask Damitra who has decided to postpone her trip back to New York.

"They aren't speaking to me."

"Don't you think it's a good idea, though, to let them know what's happening?"

"I want to tell Mr. Turner first," she says.

"Do you think that's a good idea, sweetheart?"

"He's managing my career. He's the one who's really responsible for me."

"When do you plan on telling him?"

"I've been putting it off. I guess I'm afraid."

"Would it be helpful, Damitra, if I was the one who told him?"

"You wouldn't mind?"

"Not at all."

"I think that would make it easier for me, Pastor. Thank you so much."

pray before I call.

Father God, I say, *be with me. Let me feel Your strength, Your conviction, Your sense of purpose.*

Then I dial the numbers.

His assistant answers. "He's busy," he says.

"Please tell him this is Pastor Merci, and that it's urgent."

Gates is on the line within seconds.

"Pastor, is everything all right out there? We need Damitra back in New York for rehearsals."

"Damitra is pregnant. And J is the father."

A long silence.

"I see," says Gates. "Well, this is a surprise. But life is full of surprises, isn't it, Pastor?"

"Yes, it is," I say.

"Well, just send her back to New York and we'll take care of business."

"What does that mean, Gates?"

"We'll do what we have to do."

"Please be specific."

"Ain't no way she can have this baby."

"Excuse me," I say.

"Just telling it like it is," he says.

"You're talking about killing a baby."

"You don't need to put it that way, Preacher."

"I'm just telling it like it is."

"This ain't exactly your problem. So why don't you just let me handle it?"

"Gates," I say, "there is nothing to handle except the health and welfare of the mother and the baby that's growing inside her."

"I understand your position, Preacher. Just hope you understand mine."

ncle G called me," says J.

We're sitting at the kitchen table. He's wearing a Lakers baseball cap, a Lil Wayne sweatshirt, and black Nike sweatpants. Understandably, he's feeling down.

"I presumed he would," I say.

"He doesn't think she should have the baby. He says it'll ruin her career. And mine. He says it'll throw me off the gospel circuit. He says he won't be able to book our big tour, Aunt T."

"Babies must be protected, son. That's an absolute. Careers and concerts don't mean a thing when it comes to the life of a baby. You have to believe that."

"I do believe that. But I'm not sure Damitra does. Her new album won't be released till February but the first single's out and is already climbing the charts. Uncle G will be promoting Damitra like crazy."

"Your uncle will do whatever he's going to do, J. I can't tell him his business, and neither can you. But I can tell you that you have a responsibility as a father to protect your child."

"Even before the child is born?"

"Yes, even before the child is born."

"So what am I supposed to do?"

"Own up to that responsibility. Make your love and your concern for your child known to the child's mother."

"I don't exactly know what to say."

"Listen to this song, son, and you'll know what to say."

I slip in the CD of *What's Going On.* When Marvin sings, "Save the babies! Save all the babies!" J closes his eyes and bows his head. I pray that he's praying.

"Don't Tell Me What to Do"

Damitra's single is starting to blow up. It's bangin'
everywhere. If Damitra ain't coming back here, I'm flying
to the Coast. Today."

That's what Gates Turner is telling J.

Meanwhile, my lawyer, Bob Blakey, is in L.A. for my deposition in the Golds' case against me. It's being held in a downtown
law firm at noon.

It's nearly eleven a.m. and I'm still getting dressed. The last
thing in the world I want to do today is answer questions about
my grandson's relationship with Damitra, who still has not told
her parents that she's pregnant.

In the midst of all this drama, Justine calls.

"I'm in Atlanta," she says.

"What are you doing there?"

"Working for Parker Mint."

"Lord, have mercy" is all I can say.

"What is your husband saying?"

"He understands it's a job that requires travel. He's happy that I'm happy. He knew I was getting bored working at Wal-Mart. Not enough action."

"What are you doing for Parker?"

"Anything he needs done. Traveling secretary. Girl Friday. Bearer of good news."

"What good news?" I ask. I can sure use some.

"He just got off the phone with *Billboard* magazine. The pre-release reviews of *Love Tornado* are sensational. The buzz is big. You're back, baby. You can tell that thug Gates Turner to take his gospel tour and shove it 'cause right now Parker will be able to book you wherever you wanna be booked."

"Gates Turner isn't booking me anywhere."

"You two have a falling out?"

"You can call it that."

"I knew it!" Justine exclaims. "I saw it coming! A good Christian woman like you can't have nothing to do with a knuck-lehead like him."

"I gotta run, baby," I tell Justine. "I'm late to a meeting."

"But there's more good news."

"Tell it to me fast, sugar."

"You've been tapped to appear on a BET special."

"What kind of special?"

"A celebration of music—all the different styles and all the big stars. They want you to do 'Love Tornado.' You'll be singing to millions of people all over the country! Ain't that something?"

I have to admit that it is.

The deposition is not fun. The Golds are not present but are represented by a female lawyer, a stern woman who looks at me through thick eyeglasses outlined in oversized frames of fire-engine red.

I'm asked questions I find embarrassing and outrageous.

Have you encouraged your godson to date Damitra?

Have you spoken poorly of Bishop and Mrs. Gold while in Damitra's presence?

Do you know how many girls your godson has been with sexually?

Have you found pornography in his room?

Does he frequent sexually explicit Web sites on his computer?

Have you left him and Damitra alone in your house?

Have you seen them touching one another sexually?

Have you seen or heard them having intercourse?

The answer to all the questions, of course, is no. But then the question of questions, the answer to which will certainly get back to the Golds in Dallas.

"Do you know for certain, Pastor Merci, whether your godson and Damitra have had sexual intercourse?"

I pause before answering.

"Yes," I say.

The attorney looks at me. Her left eyebrow is raised.

"How do you know that?" she asks.

"They have both told me so."

"What prompted them to tell you?"

"A conversation in which Damitra said that she was pregnant."

Were you surprised?" I ask Bob as we ride down the elevator after the deposition is complete.

"I have to say I was. You hadn't told me about the pregnancy."

"Sorry," I say, "I've been preoccupied."

"Understandably, Albertina. How is the young couple doing?"

"Confused. Afraid. Uncertain."

"Also understandable."

"Do you think my statements will have an impact on the lawsuit?"

"The lawsuit is frivolous and I expect the judge to dismiss it within a week or two. But I worry about J and Damitra."

"I've spoken to them both about their moral responsibility."

"And they hear you?"

"He does. I'm not sure about Damitra."

"I'm guessing she's in a state of rebellion—against her parents, against the church, probably against everything."

"She was raised as a good church girl, I know," I say, "and was quite obedient. She became a gospel star at a young age and, as you probably know, went on tour with her dad, singing before his sermons."

"So she's used to taking orders from powerful men," says Bob. "Even in her rebellion, I'm guessing that pattern might hold firm. Gates Turner has replaced her father."

"Oddly enough, Gates Turner is going for something of a wholesome pop image for her," I tell Bob. "My fear was that he'd package her as a teenage sex queen, but he's doing quite the opposite."

"Only because he figures that's where the money is."

"Either way, he can't have his wholesome pop princess turn up pregnant. That would ruin all his plans."

"And your plan, Albertina?"

"Stay as close to these two kids as I can. Be there for them. Be a loving presence. Keep a conversation going. I don't need to judge them and I don't need to scold them. I just need to be part of their emotional and spiritual lives."

"I suppose that's all you can do."

"If I can do that, that's a lot."

The phone rings while J, Damitra, and I are watching MTV together. The preview of her first video, *Don't Tell Me What to Do*, is about to air.

"May I call you back?" I ask Parker Mint.

"May I have a decision about your appearance on the BET music special?"

"I'll call you back in ten minutes, Parker. Promise."

The video is highly sensual, but I wouldn't call it risqué. Damitra's all-white outfit is sexy without being vulgar. The setup is that she's home singing this song to an older woman and older man who play the part of her parents. Her song says,

> *You can't run my life for me*
> *'Cause I'm the kind of girl who's gonna be free*
> *You fence me in with silly rules*
> *And it's even worse when I'm at school*
> *Do this, do that, it's the same routine*
> *Well, I'm no slave just cause I'm a teen*
> *Being free is the name of my game*
> *Can't live like you cause I'm not the same*
> *My generation is bold and brand-new*
> *So don't tell me what to do*
> *Don't tell me what to do*
> *Got to make my own breaks*
> *Don't tell me what to do*
> *Got to make my own mistakes*
> *Don't tell me what to do*
> *Things are different since you were young*

Don't tell me what to do
We're having fun
Don't tell me what to do
The world has changed
Don't tell me what to do
Everything's rearranged
Don't tell me what to do
You don't gotta clue
Don't tell me what to do
I'm gonna do what I'm gonna do
Say it again—
Don't tell me what to do
You don't got a clue
Don't tell me what to do
I'm gonna do what I'm gonna do

Damitra's voice is strong and the upbeat melody is infectious. It's hard not to like the song. The dancing is spirited, and Damitra's moves are graceful. It's no bump-and-grind. It's obviously devised to appeal to the rebellious young, and I can sure see why it's a hit.

"I have to admit that I love it," Damitra says when it's over. She's been glum these past days as we've been discussing her situation. I've sensed her mind is elsewhere, though. I can understand it. I was once a teenager in love with show business, and when the fever hits you, it hits hard. In her view, the idea of being saddled with a baby is a burden. I have pointed out that it is a blessing. "It's a joyful, wonderful thing," I say. "It takes great work and tremendous diligence, but the rewards are the most satisfying you will ever experience." I'm not sure she hears me.

But she does hear her cell phone ring. The ringtone matches the melody of "Don't Tell Me What to Do."

"Hi, Mr. Turner," she says. "Yes, I saw it. It was awesome."

Silence on her end as he speaks to her.

"What!" she exclaims. "That's incredible! That's the best, the absolute best! Sure, I'll tell J. And you'll be here next week? Well, that's perfect. Everything's working out perfectly."

She clicks off her phone and gives J a big hug.

"I've been asked to perform on a big BET music special. Mr. Turner has arranged the whole thing. 'Don't Tell Me What to Do' will be the opening number!"

"Sweet," says J. "Aunt T's gonna be on the same show. Aren't you, Aunt T?"

GiVE UP ThE LOVE

J'S DiSCiPLiNE in school does not falter—and naturally that makes me happy. He keeps bringing home good grades and good reports from Crossroads, especially from the English teacher, who praises his ability with written language. "His poetry is wonderful," she writes in a glowing letter to me. "I can see why he's so successful merging music and words."

After school, Damitra comes to our house and the two study together. I encourage that. My prayer is that they will remain a couple. I am glad when she initiates a conversation about the confusion she is feeling. I let her express those feelings without contradicting them.

"Feelings are feelings," I say. "As human beings, we're entitled to whatever feelings pass through us."

"Now I'm feeling that I'm about to ruin my life and throw away a career that most girls would kill to have."

"You're not throwing anything away, sweetheart," I say.

"You're allowing yourself to think your way through a decision you have to make."

"If I was thinking clearly, and not emotionally, I'd know what to do. If I looked at this as a practical matter, the decision would be easy. I'd see it as purely business."

"And why," I ask, "do you think you're not able to see it as purely business?"

"Well, that's the emotional part."

"And how do those emotions feel?"

"Confusing."

"I understand," I say. "I'd be surprised if it weren't confusing."

"Do you know what Mr. Turner says?" Damitra asks me.

"No, I don't."

"He says the only reason women keep babies they don't want is because of guilt. And guilt is nothing that should rule your life."

"And you agree with him?"

"Partially, yes. I stuck with my parents, who were ruling my life, because I was afraid I'd be too guilty if I ever left them."

"And do you feel guilty about leaving them?"

"No!" she says defiantly. "I feel glad."

"Well, if you're not afraid of guilt, and if guilt is the only thing stopping you, why do you think you're so hesitant about doing what Gates is telling you to do?"

"Because there's more to it than that," says Damitra.

"What's the 'more' part?" I ask.

"A baby."

J, who has been following our conversation with great care, repeats the words: "A baby." He shakes his head in wonder.

"I'm too young," says Damitra.

"I am too," says J.

"It isn't fair," says Damitra.

"It isn't right," says J.

"What isn't right?" I ask. "What isn't fair?"

"This whole situation," says Damitra.

I let silence linger for a long while. There are many things I could say, but I decide it's far better to let them live with these questions.

The questions are still on their minds the night before the BET music special. I am hopeful because no precipitous action has been taken. Damitra has not rushed off to a doctor, and J has not encouraged her to do so. They are not taking this decision lightly. The great weight of the matter is sinking into their consciousness.

Those two words—"a baby"—are much on their minds.

So is this TV show. It's a big deal for Damitra, and it's a big deal for me.

My own excitement has been bubbling beneath the surface. I've been so concerned about these children's decision that I've had too few rehearsals for my spot on the telecast. Justine has flown in from Hawaii, where, she reports, her marriage is in trouble.

"My husband suspects something," she says.

"Justifiably?" I ask.

"I think I'm in love with Parker. I know he's in love with me."

"I don't know what to say."

"You don't have to say nothing, Tina. I know what you're thinking. You look down at this sneaking around business."

"I'm looking at the dresses you picked out for me," I say. "Can't decide between the green and the black."

"Go with the black," says Justine. "Makes you look thinner."

167

"I think you're right, baby."

"I think Parker Mint is the most wonderful man I've ever met. What do you think?"

"A strand of cultured pearls might look good. You agree?"

"Along with pearl earrings, yes."

J is decked out in an Armani tux.

"Good God almighty!" Justine screams. "You are one good-looking boy! You taking your aunt to the TV show?"

"No," he says. "That's Mr. Mario's job. I'm taking my girl-friend Damitra."

'm in my dressing room, watching on the monitor, when the show opens with Damitra's "Don't Tell Me What to Do."

She looks terrific, and she brings down the house. There's no denying her power as a charismatic performing artist. She dances beautifully and expresses the spirit of her song with fire and spunk.

My song will be sung in about thirty minutes so I have time to go to Damitra's dressing room to congratulate her.

"You were beautiful, sweetheart," I say. "Simply beautiful."

She hugs me and says, "Oh, thank you, Aunt T."

That's the first time she has ever called me "Aunt T."

I look over to the couch and see Gates Turner. He gets up and greets me cordially. He's wearing a lime-green tux.

"Pastor!" he says. "I'm predicting that you'll be the big star tonight."

"Well, thank you, Gates," I say.

Just then J comes into the room. He and Gates embrace. Then J tells Damitra, "They want us back out in our seats."

He and Damitra leave me and Gates alone in the room.

"I understand preachers," says Gates. "My aunt was a preacher."

"I didn't know that."

"Preacher down in a lil' ol' church in the Georgia woods. That's where I first got religion. Yes sir, I love me some preachers."

"Glad to hear it, Gates."

"Only problem, Pastor, is that preachers got their heads up there in the heavens while life goes on down here on earth. Preachers be trippin' that way. They don't see how this life works 'cause they so worried about the next one."

"That would be a mistake, wouldn't it?"

"Big mistake 'cause it can mess up a good life and a good career both. I'd hate for that to happen, specially when we all stand to gain so much."

"Well, Gates, to be honest, I look at it this way: We've already gained God's grace, which is the most precious commodity in this world or any other. Having gained that, I'm not too interested in gaining anything else."

"Am I to believe that, Pastor?"

"I believe it, and that's good enough for me."

I leave to go back to my dressing room for a final prayer before my performance.

On the stage of the Shrine Auditorium, I blow through "Love Tornado" with what feels to me like good energy. The crowd cheers and even rises to their feet. Afterwards, I take my seat in the auditorium next to Mr. Mario, who whispers, "I'm proud of you, baby. You're a star tonight."

Afterward, at a press conference for the performers, I find

myself standing next to Damitra. A reporter asks her about the success of her hit single. She replies graciously.

"I have to credit Mr. Gates Turner, my manager, and my boyfriend, J Love. I also want to thank this lady, Pastor Albertina Merci, our wonderful aunt and mentor. We're all family."

I'm flattered by Damitra's words but also a little baffled. She sees me, J, Gates, and herself as a united family. I hardly see us that way at all. I see Gates looking to destroy a life that he views as harmful to his plan.

At the after-party at the Four Seasons Hotel, Mario and I see Gates, resplendent in a gold glitter jumpsuit. One arm is around Damitra, the other around J. He's smoking a huge cigar and holding court. Surrounding him is a cast of characters who look like they just stepped out of a gangsta rap video. I don't know their names, but most everyone else does because they're being hounded for autographs. Everyone asks to have their picture taken with them. Their outfits are extreme: superbaggy warm-up suits with slogans on them like "Heavy Hustla" and "Hating on Playa-Hating Hos." Diamond rings on every finger. Diamond grills masking their teeth. Massive chunky diamond earrings. Diamond-sprinkled Rolexes. Diamond bracelets. Diamond dollar bill medallions hanging heavy around their necks.

The pungent odor of marijuana permeates the air around them. They speak loudly, laugh uproariously, and curse without regard to who might be passing by. I see Gates Turner introducing his superstar hip-hop crew to J and Damitra, both of whom seem impressed. Gates spots me and waves me over.

"Gentlemen," he tells the assembly of rappers, "this here is a legend among legends. This here is none other than the great Albertina Merci. *Pastor* Albertina Merci. You're looking at history, gentlemen, you're looking at a woman who kicked down the door so knuckleheads like you could come on in. Give her her props. Give up the love for the one they call Aunt T."

And just like that, Gates Turner starts bowing before me. J follows suit and so do the other rappers along with Damitra.

"No, no, no," I say. "You're worshipping the wrong lady. I'm just an old singer and an old preacher. The one you wanna worship is the one you don't see."

"Preach it!" says Gates. "Listen to this lady, boys, she's plugged into the mainline and has a direct connection to the chief operator."

"We all do," I say.

"But not like you, Lady T," says Gates. "You are the one and only."

When Gates is through gushing about me, he starts gushing about Mr. Mario, who he recognizes from when Mario was a TV star. Mario sees through this man like a fish sees through water. He wants no part of Gates and urges me to move on to a reporter from *Entertainment Tonight* who wants to do an on-camera interview with me.

The interviewer is familiar with my former career and my newly resurrected career and is highly complimentary. I can't say I don't enjoy the attention. But my mind remains on J, Damitra, Gates, and all those boys blinged-out from head to toe.

That night I don't fall asleep until two a.m., some four hours past my normal bedtime. When I wake up in the morning, I go to J's room and see that the bed is still made.

He's been out all night.

What now?

HEART TO HEART

I WANT TO TALK TO him," says Mario. "I think I know what needs to be said."

"He's my responsibility," I say. "And it's not a responsibility I'm prepared to abdicate."

"You're not abdicating anything. You're merely recognizing that there are times in the life of a boy when he needs to hear words spoken by a man."

"He's a boy who's becoming a father."

"All the more reason to talk to him man to man."

"But heart to heart," I say.

"Of course," Mario agrees. "I don't know how to do it any other way. What did he say to you when he finally arrived home?"

"That Gates gave a party that went all night."

"Which wasn't over until ten the next morning?" Mario asks.

"That's what J said."

"How'd he look?"

"The way someone looks who has been out all night partying."

"And he's been asleep ever since?"

"Ever since," I say, seeing that it's now five in the afternoon.

"Well, when he wakes up, call me. I'll come right over. And when I get there, you disappear."

"I've got to be in church tonight anyway," I say.

I like this plan. Obviously my own influence on J has not been great enough to keep him in line. I feel like I've given him good moral direction. My boundaries were articulated in strict terms. To a large degree, J respected those boundaries. Until now, he has been home on time. His grades have been excellent. He has treated me with respect. His friends at Crossroads seem bright and well grounded. But he has crossed one boundary with life-altering consequences. The fact that J and Damitra are expecting a child changes everything. The further fact that they are teenagers adds to the complexity. And Gates Turner's involvement in their already entangled lives only adds to the entanglement.

Have I failed in my role as godmother?

I hardly have time to answer the question because, as J sleeps, the phone never stops ringing. Last night's BET performance has set my own career on fire. Everyone wants to photograph me, interview me, book me; everyone wants the story of this improbable comeback. *People* magazine. *Entertainment Weekly.* Even *60 Minutes* is considering a segment on me. Against the advice of my booking agent, Parker Mint, and my producer, Harry Weinger, I turn down all interviews. I cannot lose myself in a flurry of publicity, not while J is at such a critical juncture in his life. Sales of my CD, *Love Tornado,* will surely benefit from the BET show, and that makes me happy. I'm grateful for all the good work that Parker and Harry have been doing for me. But I will not lose myself in a promotional whirlwind at this stage in my life. I understand that my obligations to my church and to J come first. So all the calls remain unanswered, except one.

"Is this Pastor Merci?" asks a woman on the other end of the line.

"It is."

"One moment for Maggie Clay."

Maggie Clay is a call I must take. I say that not only because Maggie is the most popular talk-show host in the history of television, but because of our relationship. Cindy, the niece I lost to cancer, was Maggie's assistant. And because of Cindy, I became entwined in Maggie's life. She calls me her personal pastor, and I take that as a compliment. Once every couple of months she slips unnoticed into the last pew of House of Trust, where she listens to my sermon. When she is down, she'll often call me at home and ask if I have time to pray with her. I always do. She calls herself a recovering depressant, a woman who bravely fights great mood volatility. She has learned to turn not only to medical science for help with that crippling disease, but also to God Almighty. She has become a loving Christian and, as a result, she spreads goodwill wherever she goes.

"I'm calling to congratulate you, Albertina," she says. "I want to fly you to Dallas to do my show next week."

"Maggie," I say, "you're a sweetheart, but I don't think that's a good idea. I'm laying low right now."

"Laying low? You should be flying high! You've done something few artists your age have ever done. You're back in a big way."

"Unintentionally, Maggie, and not without gratitude. But the truth is that I have challenges here at home that must be met. I don't have to tell you, baby, that media blitzes can destroy anyone's peace of mind."

"I can't believe you, Albertina. You're turning down a spot to sell your CD on Maggie Clay's show?"

"No, honey," I say. "I'm reserving that spot for another day. And believe you me, I will make good on that reservation when the Lord tells me it's time."

"Pastor, I sure hope you know what you're doing," Maggie says.

"I don't, but God does."

I put down the phone and hear stirring from J's room. He stumbles out looking like hell.

"Sorry about last night," he says. "It got kinda crazy at Gates's suite."

I don't say anything. I don't know what to say.

"You going out tonight, Aunt T?"

"I'm going to church. But I want you home. Mario says he wants to talk to you."

"I'm not sure I wanna hear what he has to say," says J. "Do I have to?"

"Yes."

The next morning, sitting in the back booth of Stay Out of the Kitchen over a tofu scramble, Mario tells me about his conversation with J.

"Were you able to speak your heart?" I ask.

"I was," he says.

Mario describes the scene:

"Hey, J, I just want to listen to you."

"Listen to what, Mr. Mario?" J asks.

"Listen to what's been going on with you."

"Nothing's going on," says J. "I'm just a normal teenager."

"Hardly," says Mario. "You're a star rapper who's going with a star singer. That's not normal for a teenager."

"Is that wrong?"

"Not at all. But it isn't easy."

"Been easy for me. Been cool for me."

"So cool you got her pregnant."

"Nothing unusual about that, Mr. Mario."

"That may be, but the ramifications are deep."

"Or not."

"How can they not be?"

"We end it."

"You end your relationship with Damitra?"

"No, we end the pregnancy."

"Well, forgetting the moral arguments, you don't think ending a pregnancy has ramifications?"

"Not really."

"Son," Mario says with a sigh. "You got a lot to learn."

"Mr. Mario," says J, "I know you're a good guy, and I know you love my Aunt T, and I know you have my best interests in mind, but I gotta live my life the way I see fit."

"Ultimately we all do. But that doesn't mean you don't have to decide whose advice to take. Choosing the right advisers, running with the right folk, is one of the most important things a man can do. You guys call them posses. I just call them friends. Whatever you call them, if they steer you the wrong way, if they push you off the true track, you can be messed up for years."

"You saying I'm messed up?"

"I'm saying you're about to be."

"I don't see how you can say that."

"I say it, son, because I see it. You're sixteen and you already got a girl pregnant. You're disobeying your godmother by starting to run around with thugs."

"What thugs?"

"Those rappers."

"Rapping is a serious art form."

"I'm not arguing that, J. I'm saying those cats at the BET party—those weed-smoking bling-bling idiots—ain't into anything but what I call hypermaterialism. It's all about show, it's all about the ego, it's all about how much stuff I can get, it's all about worshipping the golden calf."

"You sound like Aunt T."

"No, I don't," Mario says. "Your godmother and I have much different views about religion. Plus that lady is a lot less judgmental than me. But I'm calling it like it is. I'm telling you that Gates Turner and his boys represent something crass and crude. You're better than all that. You're a genuinely talented artist, a genuinely talented writer."

"Those rappers can write," says J. "They can spit, but they're spittin' their own writing. And if you listen to it carefully— which I don't think you have, Mr. Mario—you'll see that they got skills you haven't dreamed of. I know you like poetry, and I appreciate how deep you are into Shakespeare, but I'm saying that the best rappers belong up there with the best poets. Their word-slinging is awesome."

"But what about the content?" Mario asks. "It's one thing to have technical skills, but if you ain't saying nothing, who cares? You can be the best movie director in the world with chops for days, but if you're turning out straight-up porn, how are you using your skills? To what end?"

"You got to define porn."

"Half the rappers out there are rappin' nothing but porn. You know it, son, and I know it too. That influences people. Influences young people. I dare say it has influenced you."

"You don't know me like you think you do."

"I'm trying," Mario says.

"No, you're not. You're preaching."

"I'm just saying get your head straight before it's too late."

"Excuse me, Mr. Mario, but I don't remember anyone appointing you my father."

"You'd listen to me if you knew what was good for you."

"I am listening, and I am looking at you, and what I see is a washed-up old actor flipping veggie burgers for a living. Is that something I'm supposed to be impressed by?"

At this point in the story, Mr. Mario turns red.

"What happened then?" I ask him.

"I slapped him across the face," he says.

"You *what*?"

"Slapped the boy. Good and hard."

"Oh, Mario," I say. "What good was that going to do?"

"Wasn't a question of doing good, Albertina. Was a matter of showing this kid he just can't run his mouth the way he wants to. Someone should have slapped some sense into him a long time ago."

All I can do is sigh. I understand Mario's frustration. I understand J's frustration. I understand my own frustration.

"What did he do when you slapped him?" I ask Mario.

"Gave me a look like he wanted to kill me. Then he just up and walked out."

"And you didn't go after him?"

"What for? I'd made my point. Had nothing else to say."

"So nothing was accomplished," I conclude.

"Nothing except that now he understands that a man can be pushed to a certain point—and then no further."

J," I say, "I'm sorry your talk with Mr. Mario didn't go well."

"He's a jerk."

"He's a good guy," I insist. "He has a good soul and good intentions and, like the rest of us, he's worried about you."

J and I are on our way back from Crossroads. I'm driving my PT Cruiser on Interstate 10, from Santa Monica back to central city L.A. The afternoon traffic is fierce, and so is J's dark mood. I try to lighten things up.

"Your teachers couldn't have had better things to say about you," I tell him. "Your English teacher thinks you should be a professional writer."

"I am a professional writer," J reminds me. "Uncle G said I should have started my own publishing firm to protect ownership of my copyrights a long time ago."

"Gates is right," I say, "but Bob Blakey told you the same thing."

"Uncle G says Bob's a toy poodle. He says an artist needs a lawyer who's a Rottweiler."

"Gates is wrong, J. Bob's strong. And tough. He's experienced in the ways of the entertainment business. After all, he represents Maggie Clay."

"Uncle G says he's old school."

"So am I," I say.

J looks down and says, "Aunt T, I have no beef with you. You came on strong when Mom died and showed me love. You took me in. I love you, Aunt T, and so does Uncle G. He gives you mad respect. It's just that some of these fools you hang with just don't get it."

"Get what, honey?"

"That young people are different than they were when you were coming up."

"I'm not sure, sweetheart. We had lots of rebels. We did lots of crazy stuff. We had our own point of view that was different from our mom's and dad's way of seeing the world."

"Well, I know you're different, Aunt T, and that's why Uncle

G and them like you so much. You had the guts to go back to singing R&B and not let the church folks tell you what to do. You do what you want to do."

"No, I do what God wants me to do. I try to be still and hear His will, J. That's what I do."

"Well, I'm hearing that voice tell me that I want to expand beyond the church too. I want to write songs that have to do with more than just praising God."

"I think that's fine. I think that's wonderful. There's no reason not to do that. I've read your compositions for English class, the ones about black history and painters like Ernie Barnes, and I can see you turning those into raps."

"That's what I was thinking, Aunt T. And when I told that to Uncle G, he got all excited and hooked me up with a label, just like that."

I stay silent. The traffic's not moving and I need to think rather than react.

"Uncle G wants me to meet the label head. He'll be over on Catalina Island in about three weeks. That's where they're shooting the next video for Damitra. Uncle G says this is the guy who heads up Tru Genius, the biggest hip-hop outfit out there. He's Australian. A business genius. Ian Spencer."

"I've read about Ian Spencer. He's an important man in the record industry."

"Will you come to Catalina to meet him with me, Aunt T? I want your opinion. I want your opinion about everything."

"I'd love to, son," I say.

"And Damitra and I have been talking about the baby. She's really been thinking about what you said. Me too. I think we want to have this baby, Aunt T. I know it's crazy, but we'll find a way, won't we?"

"God will find a way," I say. "He always does."

"Shouldn't a Preacher, Be Preaching?"

My nephew Patrick and his wife Naomi are sitting across from me. I'm behind my desk in the pastor's office at House of Trust. It's mid-March, and we're discussing something that's been bothering me since J and my revived career have consumed so much of my time: the fact that they've had to perform many of my normal church duties.

"I presume that if the congregation was unhappy, I'd hear about it," I say. "Am I fooling myself?"

Naomi, bless her heart, is not afraid to tell me the truth.

"Some members aren't happy but are reluctant to tell you," she says.

"Why is that, sweetheart?" I ask.

"Because you're something of an icon," Naomi answers, "and, to some members, you seem unapproachable."

"Me?" I ask in reply. "I'm hardly an icon. I'm just Albertina."

Patrick says, "After Naomi and I taught Bible class last Wednesday, I heard a woman say, 'Shouldn't preachers be preaching instead of appearing on BET music specials?'"

"And I'm afraid she's not alone in her opinion," Naomi adds. "You've been getting a great deal of publicity lately, Albertina, and not everyone views it favorably."

"I don't think we have to worry about those people," says Patrick in my defense.

"I do," I say. "I don't want to be sheltered from this criticism. I want to be open to it. In fact, if I don't have the support of House of Trust, then I have no right to be its spiritual leader. Let's have an open forum and invite all our members. I want to hear what they have to say. I'm going to write a letter to the congregation and encourage them to speak openly about whatever is on their mind."

One week later I arrive at the House of Trust for the forum. It's a Thursday night, and the attendance is good. I've been in prayer over this issue since Patrick and Naomi first mentioned it.

Lord, I've been praying, *You follow and I'll lead.*

I've tried to clear my mind of expectations. I don't want to be defensive. I simply want to serve God.

I look out at the congregation and begin by saying, "My introductory remarks will be brief, because tonight I've come to hear you. I know some of you are not happy that I've chosen to spend time away from you. Some may not be happy about my decision to record popular music and appear on a nonreligious television program and do nonreligious concerts. I want to hear your concerns and urge you to speak up. My mind is open, and so is my heart."

An older woman is quick to raise her hand. Her name is Ernestine Guthrie. I officiated at Ernestine's eighty-fourth birthday celebration last year, and she's someone I love dearly.

"Well, Pastor," she says, standing up, "you asked for the truth and I'm telling you the truth. When I was a little girl raised up in the church, preachers stuck to preaching. If a preacher sang, he sang about Jesus. He didn't sing about no earthly love. Now I know you're a good singer and I know you're a good entertainer, and I'm not against being entertained. I watch Maggie Clay every day because of how it entertains me. But I don't look to my preacher for entertainment, no I don't. I look to my preacher to preach the Word, pure and simple. I look to my preacher to be in the pulpit every Sunday. If I turn on the TV and see my preacher singing some love song, that don't make me feel good. Don't make me proud and don't make me happy. Am I making myself clear, Pastor?"

"Yes, you are, Ernestine, and I appreciate every word you say."

"You appreciate my words, Pastor," says Ernestine, "but do you agree with them?"

"If I agreed with them, I wouldn't have done what I did."

"Then why *did* you do what you did?" asks Ernestine, still on her feet.

"Well, let's go back to something you said, Ernestine. You were talking about when you were a little girl raised up in the church. Back then, you said, if a preacher sang, he sang about Jesus. Am I quoting you accurately, Ernestine?"

"Yes, indeed."

"Okay, but isn't it also true that if a woman had wanted to

preach in that same church, she would have been told, 'No ma'am'?"

"You're right. We didn't have women preachers back then."

"There was a prejudice. I know because I experienced it. And the prejudice said that men are more equipped to preach than women. Today we reject that prejudice. Today, thank the Lord, we embrace female preachers. Congregations like ours realize that God does not discriminate when it comes to gender or race. We are all His beloved children."

"Amen," says Ernestine, "but what does that have to do with you being out there on the same show as those rappers?"

"There are rappers and then there are rappers. Some have said that Jesus was a rapper. He talked in cadences that people found easy to understand. His words had rhythm behind them. He spoke poetry. He rapped out the message of His heart—that He came to earth to do His Father's will."

"Are you saying that Jesus would have preached on the pulpit with Fifty Cent?" asks Ernestine.

I laugh, and so does the rest of the congregation. "Jesus certainly hung out with people whom society scorned," I say. "He broke down the rules that kept people apart. And I believe our people have been hurt by rules that say a Christian can only perform so-called Christian music. That creates a division where we don't need one. What we need is unity. One God, one music, one love, one people. That's how I look at it. And that's why I sing songs of love that, to my way of thinking, honor the God of love."

Some congregants start to applaud. Others remain silent. Ernestine is unconvinced.

"You can't change how I feel," says Ernestine, "when I see you up there with thugs and knuckleheads wearing baggy pants down to their knees."

"I don't want to change how you feel, Ernestine. I'm glad that you expressed your feelings. Now I'm just expressing mine."

"How about all the Bible classes and Sunday services you've missed, Pastor?" asks Lionel Berry, a successful accountant who's a serious student of scripture.

"I don't feel good about that," I admit, "and I wish it hadn't been the case. But because of major personal and professional changes in my life coming at the same time, I've had to make choices."

"And you chose to neglect the House of Trust?" asks Lionel.

"No, I don't feel that I've neglected the church. I've missed the church. I've missed you all. But blessings brought to you by Pastors Patrick and Naomi have given me much peace of mind."

The discussion continues. I try not to sound defensive, but that's hard because, in some sense, I'm there to defend myself. For the most part, though, I allow the dissenters to say what they have to say. Some are vehemently critical. Others are openly sympathetic.

After an hour of spirited conversation, Naomi asks if she might make a suggestion.

"Of course," I say.

"For the sake of clarity, I think it would be a good idea—if Pastor Merci is willing—to ask you people, our congregants, to voice your confidence or your lack of confidence in our minister. We can do it by a simple show of hands."

"I think that is a good idea, Naomi," I say. "I'm prepared to step down if I don't have the overwhelming support of the people I serve."

"That's a courageous position," says Naomi, who goes on to ask those who would support my ministry to raise their hands.

Several hands shoot up, but not many. I'm surprised. I'm a little concerned. But after a second or two, more hands are raised, and then more, and then even more. Of the hundred or so members present, at least eighty have their hands raised.

Before Naomi can say anything else, Ernestine gets up and says, "We may fight with you, Pastor, but we all love you. Fact is, we love you so much we want to see you around here a lot more."

With that, everyone rises and starts to applaud. The applause goes on for several minutes.

I'm so choked up I can hardly talk.

"Thank you," I say. "Thank you for believing."

"SWEET SUNSHINE"

The title of the song sounds innocent, but the video itself takes another turn. Gates Turner would have it no other way. Before production begins, we are assembled around the lovely outdoor pool of a luxury hotel in the foothills overlooking Avalon, the town at the center of Catalina Island, an hour's boat ride from San Pedro, the big harbor south of L.A.

J, Damitra, and I rode the boat over together. I read the Bible while, across the aisle, J and Damitra held hands. She rested her head on his shoulder. Occasionally they kissed. I sensed something new in their relationship, a tenderness, a sensitivity, a sweetness.

"Thank you for helping us come to the right decision," Damitra said to me as the boat docked at Catalina. "I feel such peace of mind."

I gave the young girl a hug and a prayer. "May your life together reflect God's glory and wondrous grace. In His name, Amen."

It is my intention to suggest to both Damitra and J that they marry soon. Now, though, is not the time to say anything.

A few hours later, Gates is overseeing production of the video that will be shot on the lush grounds of the hotel. I overhear him tell the director, "I want the camera on that flat belly of hers. This is gonna be the last chance we have before she starts puffing up."

Gates's usual unctuous behavior toward me has taken a different turn. Instead of going out of his way to praise me to the sky, he ignores me. Surely that's because Damitra has told him in no uncertain terms of her decision to have her baby. The news hits him hard, and he credits me for messing up his plans. I credit God.

Gates is saying that "Sweet Sunshine" is going to be the biggest summer hit since Janet Jackson's "That's the Way Love Goes." Although it's late February, the Catalina weather makes it look like May, the month that the video will start rotating on MTV around the world. There are three dozen dancers and four costume changes, each one more revealing than the next—the shortest short shorts, the tiniest bikinis, the guys in Speedos, the gals in thongs. Damitra, of course, is the center of attention. She has a beautiful figure and I understand why she wants to display it. She is young. And, given her religious background, I know full well that she is still in a state of rebellion. I am just glad that she and J are together in their decision to let their baby come on through.

The video shoot takes all day. It's all about stop and start, this angle and that angle. The music from "Sweet Sunshine" blasts again and again as the dancers go through their motions. J is pleased because he wrote the lyrics to the song, his first secular composition.

Before you came round
The clouds were dark
The storm kicked up
And the lightning struck
But you showed up
Like a summer's day
And pushed the darkness
Far away
You're my sweet sunshine
My shining light
My days were dim
But you made 'em bright
You're my sweet sunshine
My every prayer
My life, my future
Sunshine everywhere!

I tell J how much I love the lyrics. I don't tell him how I think the salacious look of the video does not correspond to the sensitivity of his words. What would be the point of mentioning that now? Besides, in his loud Bermuda shorts and oversized sky blue T-shirt, Gates is in his element. He's directing the director, doing all he can to make sure that Damitra, in her many guises, is the center of attention.

When we take a break, Damitra asks me to her dressing room.

"I hope you don't disapprove of this," she says.

"I'm not here to pass judgment," I say. "I'm just here to help in any way I can."

"Mr. Turner says this is the look I need. And obviously I'm not going to have this look for very long. So I figure I have to take advantage of what I have when I have it."

"I understand."

"You do?"

"Of course."

"I was afraid you were out whispering bad things about me to J."

"I don't have bad things to say about you, honey."

"I'm just uptight because I'm going to see my parents this weekend."

"Have you seen them since you left their church?"

"No, but they finally called and invited me home to Dallas. And they also asked if J would come along. What do you think, Aunt T?"

"Reconciliation is a beautiful thing. I love the idea."

"And it's okay with you if J comes along?"

"I'd encourage him to do so. Your dad and mom have been important to his career. He owes them a great deal."

"Then you aren't angry at them?"

"Not at all, darling."

"Do you think J and I should tell them this weekend? Do you think that once they learn I'm pregnant it'll ruin everything?"

"I know you're worried about that, sweetheart, and I know it's hard not to plan. But I have a feeling that it'll all work out. New life has a way of blessing everyone."

"So you're saying wait till I'm there before I decide what to do?"

"Yes," I say. "Just follow the prompts. God is patient, and when we're patient with the challenges we face, those challenges don't seem so intimidating."

"Would you be willing to come to Dallas with us?"

"I'd be willing to do whatever you and J think is right."

"I love you, Aunt T. I hope you believe me when I say that."

"I do believe you, Damitra."

"I know we're young, and I know young love isn't supposed to last, but this is different. The very fact that I'm going to have this baby tells me it's different. I could never destroy what J and I have created."

"Would you mind if we prayed, Damitra?"

"That's why I asked you in here, Aunt T."

I take her hand and say, "Father God, how we love You! How we adore You! How we thank You for this life You have given us! The challenges are great, but Your love is greater. The obstacles are mighty, but Your grace is mightier. The fear overwhelms us, but You overwhelm the fear. You overwhelm our hearts. You flood our souls with such beauty, such optimism, such strength of purpose, such compassion and sweet forgiveness, that all we can say is, Glory! Glory be to God! In Jesus' name, Amen."

W hat did you and Damitra talk about?" J asks when I meet him later that afternoon by the pool. The video production is still in process.

"God."

"Did she tell you about seeing her folks this weekend?"

"She did."

"And do you want to come along?"

"Am I invited?"

"I'm inviting you. I think she and I would both feel better if you were there to protect us."

I laugh.

"You guys hardly need protection," I say.

"You know her parents. When they learn about the baby, they'll tear our heads off."

"Her parents are Christians, and I'm presuming that the Christ inside them will prevail."

"Even after they see this video?" J asks.

"No comment," I answer.

Just then we are greeted by a tall gentleman in a blue blazer, yellow silk shirt, white linen trousers, and penny loafers. He has a thin mustache and closely cropped salt-and-pepper hair. I'd guess he's forty.

"Hi, Ian," says J. "This is Aunt T."

"Pastor Merci," he says in his pleasant Australian lilt, "a real pleasure to meet you."

Ian Spencer looks the part of an intercontinental entertainment mogul. He orders a dry martini for himself. J and I are drinking iced tea.

"Congratulations on your new record," he offers. "I'm a soul music fan from way back."

"I'm glad to hear that, Mr. Spencer."

"And I'm glad to see you leading this young generation back over the bridge from gospel to pop. You seem to have quite an influence in that regard."

I am uncomfortable with that formulation—I see it being used by men like Gates Turner and Ian Spencer for their own good, not the good of their artists—but I say nothing. I just smile.

"I can't tell you how excited we are about J's debut rap record. Gates has some sensational ideas about themes. And I have a notion or two about how to market it. Together, we are an awesome team. Wouldn't you agree, Pastor?"

"I'm excited about my godson's talent—you bet I am. And I'm curious to see where that talent takes him next."

"Well, he can certainly rely on me and the force of my international network to ensure that his music is heard."

"Thank you, Mr. Spencer."

Sensing that I'm really not interested in prolonging our conversation, he moves on. There's something about the man I don't trust. Maybe that's because his speech is glib and his manner artificial; or maybe it's the fact that he's in alliance with Gates.

The video shoot is still not complete. At this point we've heard the hook of the song a hundred times:

> You're my sweet sunshine
> My every prayer
> My life, my future
> Sunshine everywhere!

But the sun is slowly sinking into the ocean and the sky is turning pink. The director is calling for a series of sunset shots. Now there's talk of nighttime shots.

"Got a test tomorrow," says J. "Maybe we should catch a boat back to Long Beach."

"Good idea, son," I say.

Damitra is understanding and grateful that we've been able to watch her today. She hugs us good-bye, says how much she loves us both. Gates calls J off to the side for a long private chat. From afar I see that Gates is doing all the talking and J is doing all the listening. Ian Spencer hands me his fancy card and says he'll be in touch.

As we ride down to the dock in a golf cart, we can still hear that haunting hook:

> You're my sweet sunshine
> My every prayer
> My life, my future
> Sunshine everywhere!

On the boat back to Long Beach, I'm thinking that young people in love have special challenges. Similarly, old people observing that love have challenges of their own—specifically, not to judge that love as trivial or unimportant. Maybe these two teenagers will be able to make a life together. Maybe they will be able to make their way through the confusion of the hyped-up media world and find a serene relationship with each other, their child, and God.

The water is calm under the darkening sky. The island fades in the distance. The lights of Long Beach twinkle from afar. A Scandinavian cruise liner makes her way out into the vast ocean. Seagulls swoop down from above. It may be my imagination, but I think I still hear the "Sunshine" refrain from Damitra's video.

J is silent.

"I can hear you thinking," I say.

"About what, Aunt T?"

"Damitra."

J looks at me with a smile. "You're right. I'm feeling like I shouldn't have left her. I should have waited till the shoot was finished."

"She understands that you have school."

"I suppose," he says. "But we took the boat out here together, and I wanted to ride back with her."

"There'll be other days and other rides."

"You're right, Aunt T. You're always right."

That night J goes straight for the books and stays up past midnight studying. I fall asleep shortly after him.

I can't remember them, but my dreams leave me troubled.

In the morning, the ringing phone wakes me up.

"Are you sleeping?" asks Mr. Mario.

"I was."

"Sorry, Tina, but you better get up. You better brace yourself, baby."

"What for?"

"Some bad news."

"How bad?"

"The worst news imaginable."

THE SHADOW OF DEATH

GOD DOESN'T GO AWAY. God can't go away because He is ever present and everywhere. God is the ultimate reality. He is all that is real, all that is good, all that is perpetually creative and perpetually loving. God simply *is*.

And yet, in the course of a lifetime, because of horrific circumstances, God-loving people question whether, in fact, God *has* gone away. They can't reconcile the horrors they face with a sovereign creator whose character is benevolence and grace. They wonder, they doubt, they fall into despair, they withdraw, they lose their way. They break down.

I broke down. He broke down when, less than a year ago, he lost his mother. Now he is breaking down again. His breakdown takes the same form. He isn't speaking, isn't eating, isn't crying, isn't reacting to anyone or anything.

God knows I understand.

When Mario called with the news, I gasped. I turned on the

television and there it was: a team of divers swimming through the wreckage of the helicopter and a small plane off the coast of Long Beach. The pilot of the tiny Piper plane was unlicensed and had flown erratically off course, crashing into the helicopter that was carrying Damitra and three of her dancers. The midair collision happened at one a.m., and there were no survivors. Gates Turner and Ian Spencer had elected to stay on Catalina, where a post–video shoot party went on till four in the morning. According to Gates, Damitra had wanted to get back to her aunt's house in L.A. She and J had plans to meet after he had taken his exam.

When he awoke that morning, I looked him in the eye, held his hand, and said it as quickly and plainly as possible.

"There has been a terrible helicopter accident. Damitra and three of the dancers are gone."

"Gone?" he asked.

"Gone."

His eyes shifted away from me. He went in his room, turned on the small television by his bed, saw the news for himself, and stayed silent for the rest of the day. I wanted to go in and ask him if he wanted to pray. I wanted to hold him and let him cry in my arms, but I knew he wanted to be left alone. I knew there was nothing I could say to assuage his pain.

That was earlier this morning. Since then the telephone has been going crazy. Mr. Mario came over to answer the calls—from the news services, the magazines, church members, friends, and family. I have spoken to my children and my nephew and Naomi. I have not spoken to the press. First and foremost, I must prepare myself to call Damitra's parents. This will not be an easy call, but one that I must make.

When their phone rings in Dallas, a man other than Bishop Gold answers.

"This is Pastor Albertina Merci," I say. "May I speak with Bishop Gold?"

"This is his son, Solomon. No one here is interested in speaking with you."

Damitra's brother hangs up the phone in my ear.

Mario senses what has happened. He puts his arm around me and kisses me on the forehead.

"You're a good woman, Albertina Merci," he says. "You'll get through this."

"Thank you, baby," I say. "But will he?"

I motion toward the bedroom.

"Should I talk to him?" asks Mario.

"No. Let him be."

That night I knock on the door to J's room and say, "Sweetheart, we need to talk about going to Dallas."

"I don't want to go."

"Are you sure?"

"I won't be able to handle it. You go."

"J, I think we should talk about—"

"I can't, Aunt T. I can't talk about anything now. Just go."

I go.

I'm surrounded by loved ones—Andre, Laura, Patrick, Naomi, Justine, Mr. Mario, and Bob Blakey. These people have come, not only to pay respects to Damitra, but because they are concerned about my own emotional well-being.

"You don't have to worry," I tell my children. "I am fine."

But they understand that reports in the papers and the TV tabloid shows have characterized me as something of a villainess. I am the reason, they say, that Damitra switched from gospel to pop.

"She was hesitant about leaving the church," said one of the deacons of Bishop Gold's church on national TV, "but Albertina Merci convinced her. Albertina is convincing a lot of young people to leave the church. Word has it that her godson, J Love, will be leaving soon."

"Damitra met Gates Turner through Albertina Merci," another member told *Jet* magazine. "If Damitra hadn't gotten involved with Albertina Merci, Damitra would be alive today."

"There are preachers who talk the talk but don't walk the walk," an anonymous "friend" of Damitra's told *People* magazine. "Damitra was under the influence of one of those preachers."

I can't say that the reports don't bother me. No one likes being libeled. No one likes being lied about. It's enough to deal with the tragic death of a young pregnant woman; it's enough to deal with the awful impact of that death on the father of her child; but dealing with slanderous statements surrounding the matter is another kind of challenge.

Throughout the ordeal, I lean on the Lord. I call on Him, and His response is to attend to others. To pray for Bishop Gold and his wife, Eugenia, to pray for Damitra's brother, Solomon, and all her friends, to pray for my godson, whose grief has left him immobile, to open my heart to everyone, to feel the pain, to allow the pain, to avoid turning that pain to anger and bitterness.

The church service is not easy to get through. Damitra's friends speak of her lovingly. Many of them describe the dire consequences of her leaving the church. When the elders deliver their eulogy, some take a swipe at me. They don't call my name, but there's no mistaking the reference. Bishop and his wife do not speak.

When the service is over, I approach them. I must offer my condolences. I get in the long line of people waiting to pay their respects. But when I reach the bereaved couple, they turn their backs on me. There is nothing I can say. I walk away.

As I leave the church, my family and friends by my side, I hear people talking about me, whispering behind my back, making nasty remarks.

"You should tell every last one of them to go straight to hell," says Justine as we get in the car and head back to the hotel.

"The nerve of them!" adds Mario. "They're scapegoating you for no good reason."

"They're anguished, they're hurting," I say. "They're confused."

"Will you stop being so understanding!" Justine exclaims. "To hell with those jive turkeys!"

"Uncle Gates didn't even have the nerve to show up," says my son.

"But he did send the gaudiest display of flowers I've ever seen in my life," adds Justine. "Those white lilies must have cost five thousand dollars."

"What's five thousand dollars to a gangsta like him?" asks Mario.

The conversation goes on. I want to tell them to stop gossiping. I want to tell them to stop talking. My head is pounding with the worst headache I can remember. Their remarks are only adding to my pain.

"Can we just ride in silence?" I ask.

They respect my wish and refrain from talking the rest of the way. When we arrive back at the Fairmont Hotel, I see someone in the lobby reading the latest *Us* magazine. Damitra is on the cover. The revealing shot was taken from the video. She's in a cobalt blue bikini, and the headline says, FRIENDS REVEAL DAMITRA WAS PREGNANT BY J LOVE!

I sigh.

I go up to my room and sleep. When I awake, I call my children to my room.

"I'd like us all to go to the Church of the Nazarene," I say. "I'd like to go right now."

The Church of the Nazarene is the church of my childhood, the site of my baptism, the sanctuary where my mother and father worshipped. Marianne and Norman David and their daughters Esther and Elizabeth are there when we arrive.

"We're so sorry," says Marianne when she sees me. "We know these are difficult times for you."

"They were talking about you on television, Aunt Albertina," says four-year-old Esther. "Why were they talking about you on television?"

"Hush," says Norman, feeling embarrassed.

"I don't know what they were saying about me," I tell Esther, "but what I'm saying now is that I am happy to see you, sweetheart. All I can say is that you and your little sister are the sweetest faces I've seen all day. Will you come into the church and sit next to me?"

"Yes, Aunt Albertina," says Esther. "I'll sit right next to you."

The church is deserted except for our little party. We sit on the first pew and my mind is flooded with memories of my mother. I need her presence. I need her strength. I need her optimism in the face of hard times. I need her unfettered faith.

I need my mother.

I need my father.

I need You, Lord, I silently pray. *I need You every day and every hour. I need you right now to calm my mind, to remove my anger and replace it with love, to lift my fear and let Your love move through me.*

At that moment, I feel my mother. I feel my father. I feel my God moving through me.

VULNERABLE

You've got to come on the show," says Maggie Clay.
"You're being celebrated by one camp and vilified by another. You've got to set things straight, Albertina."

"I appreciate your call, sweetheart, I really do," I tell Maggie,
"but I'm not sure the time is right."

"I *know* the time is right. This whole business about you and
Damitra and J has gone national. It's big news. I don't have to
tell you, Albertina, but in the African American community it's
stirred up that old debate about the devil's music. It's something
you need to address."

"Right now, Maggie, I need to focus on J."

"Bring him on the show with you."

"He's not ready for a talk show."

"Can't you get him ready, Albertina?"

"I can't even get him out of his room to eat. He's been there
for a week. He's doing what he did when his mom died—with-

drawing completely. He's mourning, but he's also seriously depressed. I'm worried."

"Are you getting him help?"

"I am," I say. "I have a childhood friend who's a renowned psychologist. She's coming over today. Thank God J has agreed to meet her."

"When all this gets straightened out, Albertina, I just want you to assure me you'll come on the show. I owe it to you. And you owe it to our community."

"I'm trying to work the Lord's will best as I can, Maggie. Let me just take this thing a day at a time."

F lorence Ginzburg is a lifelong friend. We've known each other longer than either of us care to remember. I consider her one of the most compassionate psychologists I have ever met. Even though she doesn't consider herself a follower of Christ—she and her husband belong to the Wilshire Boulevard Temple, a reformed Jewish congregation—Florence exemplifies all the qualities I associate with true Christians. She is nonjudgmental, deeply understanding, and, most importantly, wholly loving. I cherish her friendship. I haven't called on her professional services often, but when I have she has responded beautifully. This crisis is no exception.

She arrives at my house in the early afternoon.

"I know you don't make house calls, Florence," I say, "and I can't thank you enough for coming over."

"It's wonderful seeing you, Tina," she says. "I just wish it were under different circumstances. Is your godson around?"

"J's in his room. He knows you're coming. He wasn't wild about the idea, Florence, but he said he'd talk to you. He said he'd do it for me. I'll knock on his door, and then I think I'll run over to the church to straighten my office. I don't want J to be disturbed by any distractions."

I knock on the door. Silence. I knock again. I wait a full two minutes. Slowly I hear movement from inside. When J emerges his eyes are red, watery, and far away. He's still wearing his pajamas. I'm about to tell him to get dressed, but change my mind. At least he's willing to see my friend.

"Just put on a bathrobe, J," I say. "Florence is waiting for you in the living room."

When I get to my office at House of Trust, someone has placed the current issue of *Time* magazine on my desk. It's opened to the music section, where there's a large photograph of me and smaller photos of J and Damitra. The article is entitled "Is the Devil in the Music?"

The focus of the piece is on me and the success of my comeback CD. The article sings its praises to the sky, saying how my voice has "the urgency and truth telling of raw country blues with a slight veneer of big-city jazz." It mentions my former career as a full-time R&B singer, my big hit "Sanctified Blues," and my ordination and present work as a pastor. Then it goes into the story of J: his career as a gospel rapper, the death of his mother, and his association with me. It goes on to link Damitra to J, and J to me. "Before her tragic death," says the writer, "Damitra claimed that it was Albertina Merci who inspired her to leave the church for the more lucrative field of pop." The writer goes on to quote a number of black preachers who attack me for deserting my faith. "Just when one might have assumed that the split in African American culture between the secular and the sacred had long healed, the wound seems to have reopened. Pastor Albertina Merci, who is simultaneously active in both areas, has become the lightning rod for criticism. In fact, only last week the National Association of Christian Clerics, the most powerful and prestigious organization for African American ministers, issued a statement highly critical of the singer/preacher. Next week they will vote on Pastor Merci's expulsion."

I put down the article with a sigh.

I pick up the ringing phone.

"Pastor Merci, this is Howard Robinson, executive director of the National Association of Christian Clerics."

"How are you, Bishop Robinson?" I ask.

"Fine, Pastor. I'm calling with the results of the vote of our ruling board today."

"Is that the board that Bishop Gold heads?" I ask.

"It is."

"Then I know the results. I'm being asked to leave the organization."

"I'm afraid so."

"This has to be an uncomfortable call for you to make, Bishop, and I'm sorry that circumstances have forced you into this position."

"I'm sorry as well, Pastor. May I ask you if your letter of resignation will be forthcoming?"

"If you don't mind, I'd rather deal with this as openly and honestly as I can. I'd rather you issue a letter of expulsion. That way there will be no mistaking the facts."

"As long as you don't find it embarrassing for us to do so."

"I am embarrassed by many things, Bishop Robinson, but I'm more concerned with the truth than I am with my sense of embarrassment."

"I understand, and I admire your attitude."

"I wish I could say that I admire the attitude of your board,

Bishop, but any board that makes unilateral decisions without a fair hearing does not merit admiration. This is the first I am hearing from anyone in your organization about the matter. And what I'm hearing is that this matter has been resolved without asking me a single question."

There is silence on the other end.

Finally he says, "God bless you, Pastor."

"God bless *you*, Bishop."

When I return home, Florence is seated alone on the couch. "These are challenging times," she says.

"Amen."

"The young man has a lovely spirit about him, Tina, but there's no doubt that he's fighting depression. Deep depression. So much of his life was based on the kind of faith that his mother and you had exemplified. With his mother's death, that faith was attacked. And now with the death of Damitra and the baby, it has been renewed with a vengeance. He's furious with God."

"Given what he's been through, that's understandable."

"But he's also conflicted about that fury."

"At least he spoke with you."

"I encouraged him to express whatever anger he was feeling. I told him that voicing his anger is the first step in moving on."

"Did you mention the idea of seeing him again?" I ask.

"I don't think that's going to happen, Tina. And besides, to be perfectly frank, given your tremendous spiritual resources, you'll be able to do far more for him than I ever could."

"If he's angry at God, I presume he's angry at me."

"I don't think so," says Florence. "I didn't detect any hostility directed at you. Emotionally, he's still very needy. He needs a mother, and I don't see him rejecting a loving woman genuinely dedicated to his well-being. The basic fact, I believe, is that he's terribly confused and divided. That seems true in all areas. We spoke of his literary interests, for example. On one hand, he has started to read poets his teachers at Crossroads have been recommending—Robert Frost and T. S. Eliot. He also mentioned that your friend Mr. Mario has inspired him to read Shakespeare. J loves classic literature. He also expressed love for the gospel culture that has turned him into a star. And then there's also the hip-hop street culture that's calling to him. He's trying to reconcile all these elements. That was hard enough before this terrible accident. But after the accident, the confusion has intensified to the point where he has withdrawn. The confusion has turned to despair."

"I'm feeling it myself, Florence."

"For him or for yourself?" she asks.

"It's a fleeting feeling, I know. I know it'll pass, but this isn't an easy time for any of us."

"Tell me what's happening in your life, Tina."

I tell Tina about the *Time* magazine article and my expulsion from the National Association of Christian Clerics.

"Oh, my dear," she says. "You're dealing with an enormous amount of acceptance and rejection, both at the same time. That has to be confusing."

"God never rejects us, Florence."

"I believe that."

"God's acceptance is the acceptance that gives us the strength to go on."

"But we live in this world," says Florence, "and surely we're susceptible to the world's whims. As human beings, we're vulnerable. Extremely vulnerable. We love it when the world says that we're wonderful. And we hate it when the world says we're unworthy."

"God is worthy," I say.

"I have no doubt that God is leading you and J through this complicated crisis," says Florence. "But I also know that, no matter how deep our faith, we have difficult days. We find ourselves in valleys we have never seen before."

"The Psalms have something to say about that, Florence."

"Will you recite that psalm, Albertina? I think we both need to hear it."

I say, "The Lord is my Shepherd; I shall not want. He maketh me to lie down in green pastures. He leadeth me beside the still waters. He restoreth my soul. He leadeth me in the paths of righteousness for His name's sake. Yea, though I walk through the valley of the shadow of death, I will fear no evil. For thou art with me. Thy rod and thy staff, they comfort me. Thou preparest a table before me in the presence of mine enemies. Thou anointest my head with oil. My cup runneth over. Surely goodness and mercy shall follow me all the days of my life, and I will dwell in the House of the Lord forever."

The official UK Albertina Merci Fan Club

The offer is from England," says Parker Mint. He's calling from Atlanta. "*Love Tornado* is being released in the UK. And your old fan club is back in action in a big way."

"The offer isn't coming at a good time," I say.

"It couldn't come at a better time, Albertina. After your BET performance, sales of the CD have gone up. England is the next prime market. They still remember you from your 'Sanctified Blues' days and all those tours you made with Ray Charles. The UK has much love for you, Pastor, much love indeed!"

I thought back to my many trips to England. No one loves soul music like the British. I remember the way they greeted Sam & Dave and Otis Redding back in the sixties, the way they adored James Brown. And of course Brother Ray was a perennial favorite. He even made a movie over there playing himself. It has been years since I've been there, and I'd be lying to say that the thought doesn't excite me. But I'm not about to leave J. Not now. Not in his hour of need.

"I can't," I tell Parker.

"Are you bothered by those foolish statements from the church people?"

"I can't say those statements thrill me," I say, "but no, they're not the reason I can't go."

"Let me let you talk to Justine," says Parker. "She'll set you straight."

Justine gets on the line.

"What are you doing in Atlanta?" I ask Justine.

"Chilling with my man."

"Your man is in Hawaii."

"We split up."

"Oh, Justine, I'm so sorry."

"I'm not. He was a good man, but he found a fan who loves his singing more than I do. She's a Japanese widow with an estate in Kahala the size of New Jersey. Her husband owned half the island. So it's win–win for everyone. But what's this I hear about you refusing the UK deal? Girl, you know that's crazy. If you don't wanna tell those church people to go to hell, I'll be happy to do it for you."

"I just told Parker that it isn't the church folk, Justine, it really isn't. I feel firmly that all good music is God's music. I know I'm spreading His love and blessings, whether I'm singing 'Mary, Don't You Weep' or 'Love Tornado.' People hear Him in my voice, and that's enough for me. I'm not saying it's fun to hear all those rumors and vicious lies going around, but they aren't anything that will stop me from doing what I think is right. Besides, my own church has been beautiful in their support of me. I got to tell you, Justine, that not a single member has said anything except 'We love you, Pastor. We're behind you all the way.'"

"So what's stopping you, Tina?"

"J."

"Poor baby is still suffering something awful?" asks Justine.

"Something awful, Justine. Hardly talks or eats. He goes to school, but the teachers say he isn't his old self. He's morose, and he's angry."

"Sounds like he needs a trip to England."

"I can't pull him out of school."

"It's only a week. Besides, May in England is the perfect time to go. These people want you over there so bad I bet they'll pay for a whole entourage. You could bring J, your Shakespeare-loving boyfriend, your hairdresser Blondie, and, of course, me, your loyal wardrobe gal."

"They'd never pay for all that."

"Leave that to me and Parker. If they would, would you go?"

"I'm not sure. I need reassurance that I'm doing the right thing."

The reassurance comes later that day in an overseas phone call. One of my classmates from divinity school is now pastor of the Church of Perfect Faith in London. He calls to invite me to deliver a guest sermon. My first thought is that Parker or Justine has put him up to it.

"I don't even know who those people are," he says. "The truth, Albertina, is that I've been wanting to invite you for years and just haven't gotten around to it. Then suddenly this opportunity came up. It's a two-day revival and we need a powerful pastor like you. I know it's short notice but I'm hoping you can make it."

When I tell Justine about the invitation, she's overjoyed.

"See," she says, "I told you it's the right move. Now even God has given you the go-ahead sign."

"I'd have to get J to agree," I say.

"Don't give him a choice. Say, 'It's springtime in England, baby. So pack your bag and get ready!'"

"I don't think you can pull this off, Justine."

"You wait and see."

Later that day, the phone rings. It's Parker. He and Justine have pulled it off.

"Let me talk to J before I give you a final word," I say.

"It's the best thing for the kid," says Parker. "Change of scenery will do him a world of good."

When I mention it to J that night, he shows no enthusiasm for the idea, but neither does he express disdain.

"If you want me to go, Aunt T, I'll go."

"I want you to *want* to go, baby," I say.

"There's nothing much I want to do."

I want to go into a speech about how we must go on, how life is filled with both joy and tragedy, how he has a gift that has to be expressed. I want to say all kinds of things, but I say nothing. I know J, and I know my words will fall on deaf ears.

"I think you'll have fun," I say. "You'll love England."

J looks up at me from the meatloaf I've made for him. He tries to smile but can't quite get there. He nods his head and goes back to eating.

The planning and preparations. Selection of repertoire. Rehearsals with the band. Scheduling of CD autograph sessions, TV and magazine interviews, private parties with my fan club. I prepare my sermon for my colleague's church. I'm excited. Even thrilled. It's all falling together. My nephew Patrick will be taking over my responsibilities at House of Trust while I'm gone. Naomi Cohen is doing all she can to help out. So are my children, who are supporting me in every way. They're proud that their mother is back in the spotlight of popular music. Mr. Mario has a dozen friends he plans to see in England—associates from his days as a Shakespearean actor—and has lined up tickets to six different plays in London. On our day off, he has arranged a trip for all of us to Stratford-on-Avon, Shakespeare's home. He's as excited as I am. Everyone's excited except J. J is still morose and, for the most part, incommunicative.

The advance press is tremendous. Every day Parker faxes me articles about my upcoming tour from the newspapers in England, Scotland, and Ireland, where we'll also be playing. There are major retrospectives on my career and much praise for the new record. I thank God for these blessings and concentrate on making sure that my show will be tight and right.

The night before departure, the entourage is ready. Justine will be flying directly to London from Atlanta. Mario, J, Blondie, myself, and the band will be going nonstop from L.A. Our bags are packed. Everything is in order.

And then J becomes sick. At eight that night, he says he feels feverish. I feel his forehead. He's burning up. His temperature is 103. He can't hold down his food, and his body is shaking. I call Merv Askey, a church member who's an internist. I tell him it's an emergency. Merv comes over and examines J.

"It's a stomach flu," he says, "but not the twenty-four-hour kind. This one could take a week or so to get over. It would not be advisable to put this boy on a plane, Albertina."

"Then I'll cancel," I say.

"That's crazy," says Mario, who has come over to help me through this crisis. "You'll be doing a disservice to those who have worked so hard to plan this tour. Besides, you owe it to your fans over there. I don't think you want to disappoint them."

What Mario is saying makes sense.

I call Patrick and Naomi, who come over immediately.

"Would you mind staying with J?" I ask them. "If you could just move in here while he's recovering, I'd be grateful. When he's better, he may want to come to your house or stay here, whichever is easiest. I'm sorry I have to ask you, but this seems the best solution."

"We're happy to help out, Aunt Tina," says Patrick. "Don't worry about a thing."

"I'll come by and see him every day," says Dr. Askey.

Everyone is pitching in. Everyone is telling me that I'm doing the right thing.

Later that night I take J's feverish hand and say, "Sweetheart, I know you're hurting. And I know you'd rather that I stay with you, baby, but I have made this commitment, and I need to honor it. Patrick and Naomi are moving in here, and Dr. Askey will make sure you get better. I hope you understand."

With half-closed eyes, J nods and whispers, "It's okay. You go."

I kiss him on his forehead.

I hardly sleep at all that night.

"If Music Be the Food of Love, Play on"

Mr. Mario is introducing me to the sold-out crowd at the Royal Albert Hall, a historic and magnificent venue, the stage in London where every leading figure in the performing arts and in popular entertainment has played for the past 150 years. He's quoting Shakespeare's comedy *Twelfth Night*, after having sung my praises to the sky. He loves his job as emcee of my show and takes his role seriously. His big booming voice carries to the last row of this huge hall, and he speaks with such perfect enunciation and dramatic flair that the crowd loves him as much as they love me.

The concerts go even better than I had dreamed possible.

Old fans holding my original LPs from thirty years ago come out of the woodwork. New fans wanting me to autograph *Love Tornado* line up by the dozens. The press is adoring and the promoters sensitive to our every need. My fan club has arranged limos to take us everywhere in London and, much to my surprise, there is a small branch of my fan club in Manchester. Many of these people are, like me, in their seventies, but the thrilling part is that they're accompanied by their children and grandchildren, all of whom know my music.

Blondie is having the time of her life and Justine, who has come over with Parker Mint, sits on the front row of every concert and leads the applause.

"I hope you noticed the difference here," Justine says to me in Liverpool, where someone has shown me a picture of myself with the Beatles taken when John, Paul, George, and Ringo first came to America in the early sixties, four boys from Liverpool in love with soul music.

"There are so many differences," I say.

"The biggest difference is that here no one is saying a preacher has sold out. No one is worrying about you being a bad example. Over here they're just loving the music. And you. I think it'd be a good idea if we all moved to London."

I laugh.

"Why not?" she asks. "Parker's opening an office here. He says I could run it. And with you headquartered in the UK, you'd be bigger than Queen Elizabeth. He's been talking to promoters in France, Germany, and Italy. Tina Turner really opened up those countries for old-school soul singers, Albertina, and they'll love you over there, they really will. Why go back to a country that does nothing but talk behind your back? Why fool with all those church folk who are filled with prejudice, jealousy, and hatred?"

"I'm one of those church folk, Justine. The church is my heart. I was born in church, sang in church, went to church when I was out there singing the blues and touring with Ray Charles, studied in church, and came out ministering in church. I've never left the church and I never will."

"I've heard they have a few churches over here in England."

"Preaching in one tomorrow. Wanna come?"

"What kind of church?"

"The Church of Perfect Faith. It's mainly members from the Caribbean."

"Lots of music and dancing."

"I hope so," I say. "I studied with the pastor in divinity school back in L.A. He's Jamaican and a great man of God."

"He is handsome?"

"He has a beautiful spirit."

"That means he ain't particularly pretty. What are you preaching about?"

"Come and you'll hear."

"I'm sleeping in Sunday. After this Liverpool Saturday night concert, I'll be bushed. So what's your topic?"

"Grace," I say.

"Even for those who are sleeping in."

"Especially for those who are sleeping in."

"So we get a break?"

"God gives everyone a break."

"How about those going around blaspheming your good name? Do they get His grace?"

"Indeed they do. We're all loved, baby. We're all forgiven."

"Even if I find those people saying poisonous things about you and kick their behinds? Will I be forgiven for kicking their behinds?"

"Yes."

"So, in the name of Jesus, you're hereby authorizing me to kick their behinds."

I laugh. "In the name of Jesus, I'm ordering you to love and forgive them."

"And you can do that?"

"I can try."

Justine shakes her head in wonder. "They deserve a good butt kicking. And not an ounce of forgiveness. That's my religion."

Mr. Mario is a bit more positive on the issue of my critics.

"England has really been good for all of us," he says. "Their appreciation transcends all the problems you were having back home. This is a more sophisticated audience, Albertina. They get you. They get what you're all about. They feel your love. Just as I do, darling."

"Thank you, Mario," I say, as I kiss his cheek. "You've been wonderful to me over here. England really feels like your second home."

"Maybe it should be our first home?"

"That's what Justine was saying."

"Justine knows you well," says Mario.

"I have a church in L.A."

"And you have a nephew—and now your nephew has a wife—who are both pastoring that church with extraordinary enthusiasm and skill."

"California's my home, Mario."

"It seems like England's your second home then. I've never seen such a warm reception for anyone."

Mario's right. My sermon at the Church of Perfect Faith is received with great enthusiasm. Everyone feels the presence of the Lord. In Liverpool the spirit stays strong. The following day, the local critic writes,

Of the many comeback careers we've been privileged to witness—and that includes everyone from Charles Brown to Little Jimmy Scott to Edwin Starr—none is quite as satisfying as Albertina Merci's. Miss Merci not only sings the songs of her youth with the wisdom and patience of a master, but renders country classics—such as 'You Don't Know Me' and 'I Can't Stop Loving You'—with a heartfelt poignancy that had her adoring fans practically sobbing. Her interpretation of Bob Dylan's 'You Gotta Serve Somebody' was rendered simply: Just Miss Merci and piano. She sang songs associated with other singers—Etta Jones's 'Don't Go to Strangers' and the Staple Singers' 'Take Me There.' She did her old hit 'Sanctified Blues' and her new hit, 'Love Tornado,' but the undisputed highlight of her set was the final section in which she sang gospel. An ordained minister, Miss Merci becomes Pastor Merci the second her songs turn sacred. In that second, her artistry expands; her voice fills with hope and faith and the audience becomes her congregation. It was a rare chance to see a great artist who understands that, when it comes to singing, inspiration can come from a variety of sources.

"See what I mean?" asks Mario after reading me the review. "These people understand you."

"God understands everyone, and everyone, I believe, is looking to connect with Him. If I can facilitate that connection, I'm a happy woman and can only say, Thank You, Jesus."

Jesus, I pray that night before I go to sleep, *Protect my family, protect my friends, protect those who hear my songs and offer me such appreciation, and, dear Jesus, please protect J.*

I've been calling J every day, and the next morning, before we fly out to Dublin, I do the same.

He always says he's glad to hear from me, but his responses to my questions are never more than one-word answers: "Yes." "No." "Maybe." "Unsure." "Okay."

He's distant and doesn't give me a clue about what's going on

219

in his mind. He has refused to go back and see Florence. He says he doesn't need to. He has slacked off on his schoolwork; it's passable, but not what it was. When I speak to Patrick and Naomi, who have moved into my house, they report that he isn't saying much to them, but does seem to be getting by. Barely. His eating has not improved and, always thin, he has gotten even thinner.

"He'll come out of it," says Mario. "He did so after his mom died, and he'll do so again. In his own way, he's a strong kid."

"I like to think so."

"Right now, let's just think about the rest of this tour," Mario suggests. "In Ireland, I want to take you out to the countryside and show you where the great Irish poet William Butler Yeats is buried. I visited the site as a boy and found it absolutely enthralling."

During the plane ride to Dublin, I fall asleep.

I dream of Dallas, my mom's old church, the fur department at Neiman Marcus department store, where as a teen I was falsely accused of stealing a coat and molested by a salesman; I dream of Paris and Rome, where I am singing in baroque concert halls before kings and queens; I dream of Roscoe's Chicken on Pico Boulevard in L.A., where I am meeting the mayor of the city and the governor of the state; I dream of House of Trust, which has a new sanctuary inside the Staples Center in downtown Los Angeles; I dream of my brother, who was a beautiful singer; I dream of singing gospel songs with my siblings and singing duets with Mahalia Jackson; I dream of Billie Holiday giving me advice when I was a young girl; I dream of Mr. Mario walking me down the aisle. This last dream startles me awake.

"Is something wrong?" asks Mario, who is sitting next to me.

I smile. "Everything's fine."

"Excited about Ireland?"

"Very," I say. "Excited about everything." I put my arm through his.

Our Dublin hotel overlooks the Liffey River. My suite is charming, complete with beautiful antique lamps and mirrors, an old-fashioned canopy bed, and a bouquet of flowers to welcome me to Ireland.

I'm still sleepy from the journey and doze off for a few minutes.

The phone wakes me up.

"Aunt Tina," says Patrick, calling from California. "I'm sorry to disturb you, but I knew you'd want to know."

"Know what, sweetheart?"

"J is gone."

"Gone?"

"He didn't come home last night. Then about ten minutes ago he called from the airport. He's going to New York."

"Why?" I wonder.

"Because Gates Turner sent him a ticket."

THE WEED FACTORY

I PLAY DUBLIN that night but cancel the rest of the tour. Mario, Justine, and Parker urge me not to, but my mind is made up.

"I understand what you're saying, but my first priority is J," I say. "I've got to see what's happening with J."

I ask Parker to book me on a flight to New York. Everyone volunteers to come along with me. I tell them that's not necessary.

"I'm coming," says Mr. Mario. "Not only am I coming, I'm going to knock that knucklehead Turner on his butt. It's time someone stood up to that fool."

"Not sure that would be a good idea," says Parker Mint. "From what I know about Gates Turner, he and his crew are armed, dangerous, and crazy. Stay away, Mario."

"I agree," I say.

"I'd offer you the same advice, Albertina," says Parker.

"I'm not in the least worried. I have no plans to attack the man, and I have no fear for my safety. My concern is for my godson."

"I understand," says Parker. "But what good can you do at this point?"

"I can demonstrate my concern by showing up."

"To do what?" Mario asks.

"To be a loving presence. That's the best thing any of us can be. That's what Jesus was. That's what Jesus is."

I have many memories of New York City. The first time I played the Apollo was with James Brown. One of his backup singers was sick, and I was called in. Then of course there were the Ray Charles glory days when I was a Raelette. But the most glorious night happened when "Sanctified Blues" was riding the top of the charts. I was the headliner then, and every member of the audience felt like a brother, sister, or kissing cousin. We were all family. I felt accepted into an exclusive club of entertainers who were beloved by their own people.

Parker has been talking about booking my "Love Tornado" tour into the Apollo. I like the idea. I told him it would feel like a homecoming. I'd love to return to the Apollo. But as I sit in my midtown hotel room overlooking the Avenue of the Americas, my Bible in my lap, my mind, instead of staying on soul music, is on the state of my godson's soul.

Father God, I pray. *Let this boy's confusion lead to clarity. Protect him from darkness and let Him see Your light.*

I pick up the phone and call J's cell.

The old voice message—"Sorry I can't take your call, but please leave your number and have a blessed day"—has been deleted. The new voice message says, "Hit me back later."

I call Gates Turner's home in Brooklyn. A girl answers and tells me Gates is unavailable.

"Can you get a message to him, sweetheart?" I ask.

"Sure."

"Please ask him to call Pastor Merci."

I give my cell number and, just for the joy of the poetry and the power of the message, open my Bible to Luke 8:16, where it says, "No one lights a lamp and hides it in a jar or puts it under a bed. Instead, he puts it on a stand so that those who come in can see the light. For there is nothing hidden that will not be disclosed, and nothing concealed that will not be known or brought out into the open. Therefore consider carefully how you listen."

Consider carefully how you listen.

I listen to the roar of taxis below me. I listen to the whir of the air-conditioning unit in my room. I listen to a voice deep within me that simply says, "Do not judge, or you too will be judged. For in the same manner you judge others, you will be judged, and with the measure you use, it will be measured to you."

My eyelids feel heavy. Jet lag has caught me, and I fall into a deep sleep.

When the phone rings, I see that day has turned to night. My room is dark except for the reflection of neon.

"Aunt T, it's J."

"How are you, sweetheart?"

"I'm all right. What are you doing here?"

"I came because I was worried when I heard you left L.A."

"You canceled the rest of your tour?"

"I just wanted to make sure you're all right."

"I said I'm all right, Aunt T." There's an edge to J's voice that he has never used with me before.

"I'd like to see you."

Dead silence. I can hear my godson thinking.

"I'm in the studio."

"Wonderful," I say.

"I guess you can come down if you want to."

"I'd love to."

"But it's a different kind of scene. It's . . . well, it's not like a gospel recording session."

"Baby," I say, "I've seen many a recording session in all kinds of studios. Don't worry about me being shocked."

"Okay, as long as you know that."

J gives me the address. I shower, dress, pray, and catch a cab.

The Weed Factory is a converted meat plant on the west side of Manhattan near the docks. There's no sign on the door and the cab driver has a hard time locating the place. When he does, he wants to know if he should accompany me in. He's a dear man from Pakistan who's worried about my safety.

"Thank you, sir," I say. "I'll be fine."

The door is locked. I ring the buzzer. A deep voice replies.

"Yo."

"Pastor Albertina Merci," I say.

"You wid' the Salvation Army or somethin'? We ain't givin' to no charities here."

"I'm with J Love."

"Oh. Hold on."

Another minute or two passes before the door opens. A young girl, somewhere in her late teens, stands—or should I say slouches—before me. She's wearing the briefest denim skirt you can imagine and a skimpy T-shirt that says "Hos R People 2." Her fingernails are painted chartreuse to match her eye shadow.

She's chewing a wad of gum and smoking a cigarette at the same time.

"Mind waiting here, Miss?" she asks.

"Not at all, sweetheart."

I sit on a red leather couch. There is no mistaking the distant odor of marijuana. The walls are lined with gold records by gangsta rappers. I recognize many of the names and images. On the coffee table before me are copies of magazines—*Vibe, XXL, the Source, Black Enterprise, Black Men, Jet, Billboard,* and *Hustler.*

"Want something to drink?" the teenage girl asks me. "We got Red Bull, white wine, and Gatorade."

"I'm fine, baby," I say.

"I told J you's here. He's flowing real good right now but he'll be out to get ya."

"Thank you."

A rap song plays over the speakers in the waiting room. If I understand the lyrics correctly, they're explicit and, to any objective observer, pornographic. It's one thing when Marvin Gaye said, "Let's Get It On." It's another when the get-it-on is described in graphic terms. It's impossible not to listen, but somehow I'm able to let the lyrics go in one ear and float out the other.

A few minutes later, J arrives. His eyes are red, his lips curled up in a hazy faraway smile. He's stoned.

"Hey, Aunt T."

"Hi, sweetheart," I say.

We hug, and the unmistakable smell of weed is all over him. That smell is intensified when he leads me into the control booth.

"I told the cats to air out the room, Aunt T," he says, "but it's still a little funky."

It's a *lot* funky.

The engineer behind the big board is a big man wearing an oversized white T-shirt and a Mets baseball cap turned to the side. His assistant, an Asian teenager with colorful tatoos running up and down his arms, brings me a chair.

"Thank you, young man," I say.

"This is my godmother, everybody," says J. "This is the woman who looks after me."

Everyone nods in my direction. Everyone seems stoned.

"Is Gates here?" I ask.

"He just left," says J. "He'll be back later. Well, I better get back out there and do my thing."

"Please, sweetheart. I don't want to interrupt. I just want to hear what you're doing and thank you for allowing me to listen."

J goes from the control booth into the studio itself, where he stands before a mic. He has some words written down on a yellow legal pad. He signals the engineer to start the prerecorded track—a hypnotic and, to my mind, mournful groove—over which he raps out his story:

> *Hey, God, I got some questions*
> *I wanna ask you now*
> *If you got a minute, God,*
> *Wanna ask you how*
> *In hell should we believe*
> *While there's so much crap*
> *We can't conceive*
> *Like babies dying*
> *Before they've born*
> *And suffering children*
> *Who've done no wrong*
> *Like freaky accidents*
> *That kill the good*

And killer drugs
Wiping out the hood
Like evil-doers grabbing the gold
Who go unpunished
And grow more bold
So what I'm saying
From my heart
Is that my heart is broken
And that's just the start
See, I've given up
On believing in you
And I'm here to say
I'm breaking through
Can you hear me, God?
Or have you gone away?
Can you hear me, God?
What can you say?
Can you hear me, God?
I need explanations
Can you hear me, God?
For my messed-up situation
Can you hear me, God?
Is this how you play the game?
Can you hear me, God?
Or are you just a name?
Can you hear me, God?
Are you really real?
Can you hear me, God?
What's the deal?
Can you hear me, God?
Are you just a stranger?
Can you hear me, God?

Can you hear my anger?
Can you hear me, God?
I'm not understanding
Can you hear me, God?
Your commanding
Can you hear me, God?
Why did you destroy
Can you hear me, God?
What I enjoyed?
Can you hear me, God?
Can you tell me why
Can you hear me, God?
I've believed a lie
Can you hear me, God?
What's it all about?
Can you hear me, God?
I'm down and I'm out.
Can you hear me, God?
What's it all about?
Can you hear me, God?
I'm down and I'm out.
Can you hear me, God?
What's it all about?
Can you hear me, God?
I'm down and I'm out.

When he's through, he comes back into the sound booth and asks to hear a playback. He does not ask my opinion and I don't give it. As he listens to his voice, his eyes are closed.

Just as the song ends, the door opens and Gates Turner walks through. He's wearing a gold lamé hoody, black silk workout pants, and a baseball cap with gold letters that spell out "Da

Man." He's smoking the longest cigar I've ever seen. Accompanying him are two young women who look like they could have been in Ike and Tina Turner's band back in the days of the Ikettes.

"Pastor!" he says when he sees me. "Good to see you! Have you been offered a refreshment?"

"I have, Gates. I'm fine."

"Well, let's hear what our boy has been up to. I don't know if he told you, but Ian Spencer is putting up a fortune to promote J's debut release on Tru Genius. He thinks he's going to be bigger than Biggie. I do too. That's why I'm producing it myself. If I'm wrong about this, I'm wrong about everything. But I know I'm right. See, J's expressing what all the kids out there are feeling. Ain't that right?"

I smile and say nothing.

The engineer hits a button and we hear the playback again. As the sound reverberates through the room, the huge bass bottom booming loudly enough to wake the dead, Gates has his arm around J. He rocks back and forth to the intoxicating beat. His girlfriends do a little dance.

When it's through, he says, "Dawg, it's dope, but the thing needs more attitude. More anger. Go back out there and think about what you've been through. Don't hold back. Say what you got to say, boy. Bite off dem words. Spit like you mean it."

J takes the direction and does it again. This performance does reveal another layer of anger that wasn't expressed earlier.

"You getting there, dawg. You getting there," says Gates. "Now hit it one more time and this time get crazy with the thing! This is you, baby! This is your shot!"

After the third time, Gates is convinced he has a winner.

"Let's look at those other titles you've been writing and see what we wanna break off tomorrow," says Gates.

J reads off his titles: "Get It While You Can," "Need It Now," "Good to Be Bad," "Crazy in Bed," "Doing the Do."

When they're through discussing their work schedule, Gates asks me whether I'd like a ride back to my hotel. I would.

Gates's Escalade is waiting. I sit in the passenger seat next to the driver. In the back are Gates, J, and the two Ikettes. Out of respect to me, no one is smoking or drinking. Occasionally, Gates will slip out a curse word, but when he does he's quick to apologize.

When we reach the Hilton, I get out. J gets out with me.

"I'll walk you in, Aunt T."

"That won't be necessary, baby."

"When are you going back to L.A.?"

"I'm thinking of sticking around New York for a while. If you don't mind, I'd like to watch you finish your record."

"You sure?"

"Only if you don't mind."

I can see my remarks have confused him. I can see that he's still stoned.

"I don't mind," he finally says.

"Then we'll talk tomorrow, sweetheart."

I kiss him on his cheek, thank Gates and his driver for the ride, tell the girls goodnight, and go on my way.

Where Are You, God?

Ray Charles told me something I've never forgotten: never try to deal with someone when they're intoxicated.

"Wait till the next morning when they're all sobered up," Ray would say. "Then you got a shot at making your point. If they're wasted, just leave 'em alone."

Given the circumstances at the studio last night, I knew it was best to remain quiet. I appreciated that, once I was there, the guys had put away the pot and didn't drink in my presence. I appreciated the respect. But I also knew that, given their altered consciousness, any remarks I made would have minimal influence.

None of this shocked me. I grew up in an era when songs about intoxicants were all the rage. I'm talking about the early hits like Amos Milburn's "Bad, Bad Whiskey" and "One Scotch, One Bourbon, One Beer," Stick McGhee's "Drinking Wine, Spo-

Dee-O-Dee." Later on, when I had become a professional performer, Ray Charles had a smash single called "Let's Get Stoned." The rhythm and blues music that I love so much is filled with references to the high life that party people love to live. This will always be the case.

I also was hardly shocked to see artists, even my godson, recording while under the influence. After all, I've been around. Now I'm not justifying any of this. I've never been a doper and never will be. I watched what heroin did to so many wonderful musicians. It ruined careers and ruined lives. While it's certainly not true in every case, lighter intoxicants can lead to heavier ones, and the heavier ones are undoubtedly killers. I'd be lying if I didn't say that I'm alarmed to see my godson working in an environment where dope is widespread.

But what do I do about it?

Mario already had his confrontation with J, and what good did it do? Mario spoke his mind to J about his opinion of Gates Turner, and what good did that do?

J is working with Gates. Gates has hooked him up with a major label. The train has already left the station.

I call J early in the afternoon.

"What's up, Aunt T?" he asks.

"Thought we might have an early dinner before you go back to the studio tonight," I say.

"Okay."

"They've redone One Hundred Twenty-fifth Street up in Harlem," I say. "I'd like to see all the new stores. Would you mind meeting me up there?"

"Isn't that where the Apollo is?"

"Exactly."

"I've never seen it."

"Well, this is your chance. Can you have your driver pick me up and we'll drive up there together?"

"No problem."

When I get into the Escalade, I see that J is wearing a black workout suit with a piece of gold-and-diamond jewelry around his neck in the shape of the letter "J." He notices me noticing it.

"Gift from Uncle G," he says.

"Beautiful gift," I say. "I presume the J is for Jesus."

J smiles, and the Escalade, driven by the same man from last night, a beefy brother who has the look of a security guard, takes off into Manhattan's midtown traffic.

The car radio, which sounds like it has at least twelve speakers, is booming last night's rap, "Can You Hear Me, God?" The hook plays again and again:

> *Can you hear me, God?*
> *What's it all about?*
> *Can you hear me, God?*
> *I'm down and I'm out.*

After hearing the song the fourth or fifth time, J turns it off. I have the feeling he's playing it to challenge me, to tell me that this is his song, his point of view, his stand against what he sees as the world's injustice.

I still don't say a word.

Traffic hits a standstill on Broadway as we inch our way uptown.

"Okay, Aunt T," J finally says. "You might as well tell me. You hate it, don't you?"

"You really want my opinion?"

"It won't change anything I'm doing, but yes, I want to hear what you think."

"I love it."

"Oh, come on, Aunt T, be straight."

"I'm straight as a gate, baby, and I'm speaking from my heart. I love your song. I hear it as a prayer."

"What kind of prayer are you talking about?"

"When you talk to God, it's always a prayer. And this song is nothing but a conversation with God. It's a beautiful conversation, sweetheart, because you're absolutely sincere. You're questioning God."

"And that doesn't bother you?"

"How could it bother me, baby? You have doubts, and that's the truth. There is no faith without doubts. If you just plain believe without questioning that belief, the belief is weak. Belief has to be challenged. Nothing wrong with that."

"I'm surprised," says J. "I would have thought you'd see it as a sacrilege."

"Look, sweetheart, long time ago I realized that the conversations people have with God are their business, not mine. In this case, you're opening up that conversation to the world. So it's a privilege for us to hear that conversation. But the important thing is that you're communicating with the Lord. You're letting Him know how you feel. The fact that you question Him and challenge Him doesn't bother me in the least. He can take all the questioning and challenging you got. He's God Almighty. As long as you stay in touch, you'll be fine. I'm just so grateful that you're staying in touch with Him. I'm so thankful that you and He are maintaining a fellowship. Keep on doubting, keep on questioning, keep on pouring out your heart, sweetheart, keep on rapping, keep on knocking on His door and asking whether He's there or not. Because one thing I'm as sure of as the air I breathe: He's there. He's here. He's everywhere."

J falls into a deep silence.

In a tentative voice, the driver says, "Pardon me for saying so, Pastor, but what you said is deep. Real deep. I'm feeling blessed to be driving this car and hearing your words."

"Well, thank you, son," I say. "But those words aren't mine. They're just coming through me. I'm just being used by the Original Rapper Himself."

"Praise God," says the driver.

My friend, the manager of the Apollo, has opened the door for us. We're standing in the lobby. The ghosts are with us. The ghosts are singing inside our heads. Ella, Sarah, Billie. Dizzy, Ray, B.B., James Brown, Jackie Wilson, Little Willie John. These are the giants whose sounds are eternal. We see them before us.

J looks around in awe.

"Did you know them?" he asks.

"Yes," I say. "Some better than others."

"What were they like?"

"They were like you, baby. They were artists. Their heads were filled with creative ideas. Their hearts were filled with love. They wanted to bring out that love and give it to the people."

J stays silent a long while.

We walk into the empty auditorium and look at the empty stage. I see myself, as a young woman, singing on that stage. I remember the feeling. I remember the love. I look over at my godson and see that his eyes are filling with tears.

"My mother sang on that stage, didn't she?" he says.

"Indeed she did, sweetheart. She sang beautifully."

We eat at Sylvia's on Lenox Avenue. I think about discussing J's use of pot, but decide that the timing is not right. He still has the Apollo in his head and to chastise him would kill his mood.

"I think I feel like going to the studio," he says after eating an omelet. "Would you come with me?"

"I'd love to, baby."

Soon as we arrive at the Weed Factory, he breaks out a yellow pad and starts rewriting his raps.

"Get It While You Can" becomes "Think While You Can."

"Need It Now" becomes "The Need Is Now."

"Crazy in Bed" becomes "Crazy in the Head."

"Good to Be Bad" becomes "What's Good? What's Bad?"

"Doing the Do" becomes "What Can You Do?"

Answers become questions. The certainty of sexual conquest is replaced with the uncertainty of temporary pleasure.

A new song, "The Apollo," says, "Mama was there, singing with Ray, and she still sings to me, each and every day."

The final song is called "D."

"She showed me love, and left too soon, but the memories I cherish, can never be ruined."

When I look up, it is three a.m. J has been writing nearly twelve hours straight. Gates has come and gone, wanting to know what's going on.

"Aunt T is just helping me with some rewrites," says J.

Gates looks at us skeptically but leaves us alone.

Occasionally J reads a verse to me, asking what I think.

"You're a poet, baby," I say. "Just keep flowing."

The phone rings the next morning at eight a.m. I'm still asleep.

"I had a dream," says Mr. Mario.

I yawn and realize it's only five a.m. in L.A.

"What are you doing up so early, honey?" I ask.

"The dream woke me up," says Mario.

"What was the dream about?"

"Jesus."

My heart starts racing. Now I'm wide awake. "What about Jesus, baby?" I ask.

"He spoke."

Mr. Mario's voice, normally booming, is subdued and soft.

"What did He say?" I ask.

"One word," says Mario. "Only one word."

"What was it?"

"Believe."

ThE MaGGiE CLaY ChRiSTMaS ShoW

AS ThE TOP-RaNKED talk-show host on television, Maggie Clay knows what she's doing. Every Christmas she has a show centered on what she calls the most heartwarming story of the year.

This year her guests are J, Mario, my nephew Patrick, his wife, Naomi, and me.

"Our theme," says Maggie, "is reconciliation."

The six of us are sitting in a semicircle. I look out at the studio audience in Maggie's Dallas studio and see, seated on the front row, Marianne and Norman David along with their daughters Esther and Elizabeth. The presence of the David family is a comfort and a blessing.

Tall and thin, Maggie is dressed in an elegant black wool pantsuit. Mr. Mario is wearing a blue blazer. Patrick's style, like Naomi's, is low key: he's in subtle gray pinstripes, her dress is an elegant shade of mauve. My dress is silver. It's a vintage piece that was part of my wardrobe from the sixties. I always save my old clothes because I know they'll eventually come back in fashion.

Maggie starts off with Patrick and Naomi, who tell the story of their stormy courtship, their marriage, their conflicts, and their eventual reconciliation in Christ.

Mr. Mario is next. Mr Mario is ready. He loves being on camera and he loves speaking. He knows he's articulate. And of course he can't resist quoting *Hamlet:* "There are more things in heaven and earth, Horatio, than are dreamt of in your philosophy."

"And what are those dreams you never thought possible?" Maggie asks.

"First of all, that this old atheist you're looking at—this stubborn, lifelong, absolutely committed atheist—would be saying on national television that there is a God who can change your life. I say that because He changed mine."

"How?" Maggie wants to know.

"Well, by putting me in a position to marry this woman sitting next to me."

"Wait a minute, Mario," I say. "There's a condition. We must continue our courtship until our hearts are united as one."

"If Mario agrees to your conditions," says Maggie, "when will the marriage take place?"

"I'm in no hurry," I say. "We have a wonderful friendship, but you just can't rush a righteous courtship."

"Amen," says Maggie before turning to J with her next question: "Your new record, *God, Can You Hear Me?* is currently number one, supplanting even the hottest hip-hop records by rappers with explicit lyrics. How do you explain that, J?"

J is resplendent in a super-sharp kelly green three-piece suit.

"I can't explain it," he says. "I can only love it."

Maggie asks him how the record evolved. He tells the story about his epiphany at the Apollo, and how he took his original lyrics and expanded them. He talks about how hip-hop can—and does—address the important questions facing young people. He also talks about getting high, and how that only confused rather than clarified his thoughts. He says, "The idea is to go deeper."

"J's concept was deep to begin with," I add. "He began this record as a conversation with God, and the conversation just got longer."

"Does it bother you, Albertina, that the beats—the rhythms of the record—are hard-core hip-hop?"

"I like the beats, Maggie," I say. "There are no bad beats, no bad rhythms. The rhythms we feel are the forces of creativity."

"God," says Mario, "provides the cosmic groove."

"And how do you answer your critics who say that you've been playing both sides of the street?" Maggie asks me.

"I don't answer them," I say. "I love them. I love that they, like me, are engaged in a conversation with God. Their conversation is different from mine, but that's okay. I can't control them and they can't control me. I don't question their love of the Lord. I know that, like all of us, they're caught up in what I call the 'Love Tornado.' God's love is so powerful, so overwhelming, it can push us in different directions."

"Then how do you know that you're being pushed in the right direction?"

"Well, Maggie," I say, "when you look at a family like this one and see how we've been brought together, you understand that this is good, this is right, this is the sure-enough work of God."

ACKNOWLEDGMENTS

Proverbs 3:6 states, "Acknowledge God in all our ways and He [God] will direct our paths."

I acknowledge and thank God for the ability, the peace, His wisdom and knowledge to do this book project with you, for without Him it would not have been done. To God be the glory.

—Mable

All praises to God. And all thanks to the wonderful Mable John, Janet Hill, Christian Nwachukwu, Jr., Geoff Martin, David Vigliano, Mike Harriot, Kirby Kim, Roberta, Alison, Jessica, Charlotte Pearl, Alden, James, Henry, Jim, Alan, Harry, Leo, and forever friends Richard Freed and Richard Cohen.

—David

Readers' Guide

1. Can you imagine a situation where Justine's behavior, given her personality, might cross the line in Albertina's eyes? How do you let your own friends be themselves, imperfections and all?

2. How would you have dealt with J Love if you were in Albertina's position? Are love and tolerance always the right course of action, or are there times when stricter discipline is necessary?

3. How do Mr. Mario's ideas of structure, discipline, and moral value conflict with Albertina's? Furthermore, how do they correlate to his temperament and how do they affect his spiritual condition?

4. Are J and Damitra too young for the fame and attention they experience in the story? Is there a point in circumstances like theirs that youth is exploited no matter what?

5. Naomi has a conversion of faith during the course of the story. Given the pressure Patrick puts on Naomi to accept Christ as Lord, savior, and the only true path to heaven, is her conversion genuine? Is it possible to have a conversion of faith and still hold on to one's cultural heritage?

6. What does Gates Turner represent in this story? How is he different from Bishop Gold?

7. We get to meet Eugenia Gold in the new installment of Albertina chronicles. What was your first impression of her? How would you describe her as a wife or as a mother?

8. The more J is exposed to the pitfalls of materialism, promiscuity, and duplicity, the more he succumbs to temptation and the more at risk he becomes. How much of this influence is external? How much of a factor does the tragedy of losing his mother play in his circumstances? Should J be held accountable for any of his own choices and behavior?

9. When Damitra dies, J's grief is directed toward God in the form of anger. How does his emotional turmoil conflict with the spiritual verse (Psalm 23) Albertina references in the wake of such tragedy?

10. Despite her deep commitment to and reliance upon her faith, Albertina also sees the merit and value of modern therapy in times of crisis. What common ground would she say that they share?

11. J's rap, *"Can You Hear Me, God?"* puts into words the turmoil he feels given the tragedies he faces in the story. What similar

crises of faith does Albertina have? Can you imagine events in her life when she would have questioned God with the same skepticism J does now?

12. Albertina's guiding philosophy toward her adversaries is to try to love their best and not fear their worst. What experience have you had in your own life with this as a guiding principle?

ABOUT THE AUTHORS

MABLE JOHN is the author of *Sanctified Blues* and *Stay Out of the Kitchen!* and was the first female recording artist for Motown, the lead "Raelette" for Ray Charles from 1968 to 1976, and a successful solo artist for Stax/Volt. She's now an ordained minister with a doctorate in counseling. Dr. John appeared in the John Sayles movie *Honeydripper*. She is also featured on the *Stax 50th Anniversary Celebration* CD boxed set.

DAVID RITZ is the coauthor of *Sanctified Blues* and *Stay Out of the Kitchen!* with Dr. Mable John and the author of *Messengers: Portraits of African American Ministers, Evangelists, Gospel Singers, and Other Messengers of the Word*, as well as biographies of Marvin Gaye and jazz singer Jimmy Scott. He has also coauthored autobiographies of Ray Charles, B.B. King, Aretha Franklin, Smokey Robinson, and other musicians. He lives in Los Angeles, California.

When the Lord works in mysterious ways, it's up to Albertina Merci to find out why

Albertina Merci, singing backup with soul legends Ray Charles and James Brown, lets her voice step off the stage and into the hearts of thousands of adoring fans. But one night, when she receives a call from the Lord that leaves her contralto on mute, her stage becomes a pulpit and Albertina begins her path to pastor. With wit, charm, and grace, Pastor Merci gets to the bottom of life's little mysteries, both human and divine.

Everyone's favorite blues singer-turned-evangelist finds her romantic life heating up with the possibility of new love—with two very different men. Deciding between two budding romances is not the only challenge Albertina faces. She also has to battle to save her little church in LA from a mega-church pastor who wants not only the land where her church sits, but her nephew's loyalty as well.

Broadway Books • Available wherever books are sold • www.broadwaybooks.com

Printed in the United States
by Baker & Taylor Publisher Services